MELMOTH THE WANDERER

AND

MELMOTH RECONCILED

MELMOTH THE WANDERER

AND

MELMOTH RECONCILED

CHARLES ROBERT MATURIN
AND HONORÉ DE BALZAC

Introduction by Julian Hawthorne

WILDSIDE PRESS

Published by Wildside Press LLC.
www.wildsidebooks.com

CONTENTS

INTRODUCTION TO MELMOTH THE WANDERER

JULIAN HAWTHORNE

Balzac likens the hero of one of his short stories to "Moliere's Don Juan, Goethe's Faust, Byron's Manfred, Maturin's Melmoth—great allegorical figures drawn by the greatest men of genius in Europe."

has remained so deep in oblivion, appears immediately on a glance at the original. The author, Charles Robert Maturin, a needy, eccentric Irish clergyman of 1780-1824, could cause intense suspense and horror—could read keenly into human motives—could teach an awful moral lesson in the guise of fascinating fiction, but he could not stick to a long story with simplicity. His dozens of shifting scenes, his fantastic coils of "tales within tales" sadly perplex the reader of "Melmoth" in the first version. It is hoped, however, that the present selection, by its directness and the clearness of the story thread, may please the modern reader better than the involved original, and bring before a wider public some of the most gripping descriptions ever penned in English.

MELMOTH THE WANDERER

CHARLES ROBERT MATURIN

John Melmoth, student at Trinity College, Dublin, having journeyed to County Wicklow for attendance at the deathbed of his miserly uncle, finds the old man, even in his last moments, tortured by avarice, and by suspicion of all around him. He whispers to John:

"I want a glass of wine, it would keep me alive for some hours, but there is not one I can trust to get it for me—they'd steal a bottle, and ruin me."

John was greatly shocked. "Sir, for God's sake, let *me* get a glass of wine for you."

"Do you know where?" said the old man, with an expression in his face John could not understand.

"No, Sir; you know I have been rather a stranger here, Sir."

"Take this key," said old Melmoth, after a violent spasm; "take this key, there is wine in that closet—Madeira. I always told them there was nothing there, but they did not believe me, or I should not have been robbed as I have been. At one time I said it was whisky, and then I fared worse than ever, for they drank twice as much of it."

John took the key from his uncle's hand; the dying man pressed it as he did so, and John, interpreting this as a mark of kindness, returned the pressure. He was undeceived by the whisper that followed—"John, my lad, don't drink any of that wine while you are there."

"Good God!" said John, indignantly throwing the key on the bed; then, recollecting that the miserable being before him was no object of resentment, he gave the promise required, and entered the closet, which no foot but that of old Melmoth had entered for nearly sixty years. He had some difficulty in finding out the wine, and indeed stayed long enough to justify his uncle's suspicions—but his mind was agitated, and his hand unsteady. He could not but remark his uncle's extraordinary look, that had the ghastliness of fear superadded to that of death, as he gave him permission to enter his closet. He could not but see the looks of horror which the women exchanged as he approached it. And, finally, when he was in it, his memory was malicious enough to suggest some faint traces of a story, too horrible for imagination, connected with it. He remembered in one moment most distinctly, that no one but his uncle had ever been known to enter it for many years.

Before he quitted it, he held up the dim light, and looked around him with a mixture of terror and curiosity. There was a great deal of decayed and useless lumber, such as might be supposed to be heaped up to rot in a miser's closet; but John's eyes were in a moment, and as if by magic, riveted on a portrait that hung on the wall, and appeared, even to his untaught eye, far superior to the tribe of family pictures that are left to molder on the walls of a family mansion. It represented a man of middle age. There was nothing remarkable in the costume, or in the countenance, but *the eyes*, John felt, were such as one feels they wish they had never seen, and feels they can never forget. Had he been acquainted with the poetry of Southey, he might have often exclaimed in his after- life,

"Only the eyes had life,
They gleamed with demon light."
  —Thalaba.

From an impulse equally resistless and painful, he approached the portrait, held the candle toward it, and could distinguish the words on the border of the painting—Jno. Melmoth, anno 1646. John was neither timid by nature, nor nervous by constitution, nor superstitious from habit, yet he continued to gaze in stupid horror on this singular picture, till, aroused by his uncle's cough, he hurried into his room.

The old man swallowed the wine. He appeared a little revived; it was long since he had tasted such a cordial— his heart appeared to expand to a momentary confidence. "John, what did you see in that room?"

"Nothing, Sir."

"That's a lie; everyone wants to cheat or to rob me."

"Sir, I don't want to do either."

"Well, what did you see that you—you took notice of?"

"Only a picture, Sir."

"A picture, Sir!—the original is still alive."

John, though under the impression of his recent feelings, could not but look incredulous.

"John," whispered his uncle. "John, they say I am dying of this and that; and one says it is for want of nourishment, and one says it is for want of medicine—but, John," and his face looked hideously ghastly, "I am dying of a fright. That man," and he extended his meager arm toward the closet, as if he was pointing to a living being; "that man, I have good reason to know, is alive still."

"How is that possible, Sir?" said John involuntarily, "the date on the picture is 1646."

"You have seen it—you have noticed it," said his uncle. "Well,"—he rocked and nodded on his bolster for a moment, then, grasping John's hand with an unutterable look, he exclaimed, "You will see him again, he is alive." Then, sinking back on his bolster, he fell into a kind of sleep or stupor, his eyes still open, and fixed on John.

The house was now perfectly silent, and John had time and space for reflection. More thoughts came crowding on him than he wished to welcome, but they would not be repulsed. He thought of his uncle's habits and character, turned the matter over and over again in his mind, and he said to himself, "The last man on earth to be superstitious. He never thought of anything but the price of stocks, and the rate of exchange, and my college expenses, that hung heavier at his heart than all; and such a man to die of a fright—a ridiculous fright, that a man living 150 years ago is alive still, and yet—he is dying." John paused, for facts will confute the most stubborn logician. "With all his hardness of mind, and of heart, he is dying of a fright. I heard it in the kitchen, I have heard it from himself—he could not be deceived. If I had ever heard he was nervous, or fanciful, or superstitious, but a character so contrary to all these impressions—a man that, as poor Butler says, in his 'Remains of the Antiquarian,' would have 'sold Christ over again for the numerical piece of silver which Judas got for him,'—such a man to die of fear! Yet he *is* dying," said John, glancing his fearful eye on the contracted nostril, the glazed eye, the drooping jaw, the whole horrible apparatus of the facies Hippocraticae displayed, and soon to cease its display.

Old Melmoth at this moment seemed to be in a deep stupor; his eyes lost that little expression they had before, and his hands, that had convulsively been catching at the blankets, let go their short and quivering grasp, and lay extended on the bed like the claws of some bird that had died of hunger—so meager, so yellow, so spread. John, unaccustomed to the sight of death, believed this to be only a sign that he was going to sleep; and, urged by an impulse for which he did not attempt to account to himself, caught up the miserable light, and once more ventured into the forbidden room—the *blue chamber* of the dwelling. The motion roused the dying man—he sat bolt upright in his bed. This John could not see, for he was now in the closet; but he heard the groan, or rather the choked and gurgling rattle of the throat, that announces the horrible conflict between muscular and mental convulsion. He started, turned away; but, as he turned away, he thought he saw the eyes of the portrait, on which his own was fixed, *move*, and hurried back to his uncle's bedside.

Old Melmoth died in the course of that night, and died as he had lived, in a kind of avaricious delirium. John could not have imagined a scene so horrible as his last hours presented. He cursed and blasphemed about three halfpence, missing, as he said, some weeks before, in an account of change with his groom, about hay to a starved horse that he kept. Then he grasped John's hand, and asked him to give him the sacrament. "If I send to the clergyman, he will charge me something for it, which I cannot pay—I cannot. They say I am rich—look at this blanket—but I would not mind that, if I could save my soul." And, raving, he added, "Indeed, Doctor, I am a very poor man. I never troubled a clergyman before, and all I want is that you will grant me two trifling requests, very little matters in your way—save my soul, and (whispering) make interest to get me a parish coffin—I have not enough left to bury me. I always told everyone I was poor, but the more I told them so, the less they believed me."

John, greatly shocked, retired from the bedside, and sat down in a distant corner of the room. The women were again in the room, which was very dark. Melmoth was silent from exhaustion, and there was a deathlike pause for some time. At this moment John saw the door open, and a figure appear at it, who looked round the room, and then quietly and deliberately retired, but not before John had discovered in his face the living original of the portrait. His first impulse was to utter an exclamation of terror, but his breath felt stopped. He was then rising to pursue the figure, but a moment's reflection checked him. What could be more absurd, than to be alarmed or amazed at a resemblance between a living man and the portrait of a dead one! The likeness was doubtless strong enough to strike him even in that darkened room, but it was doubtless only a likeness; and though it might be imposing enough to terrify an old man of gloomy and retired habits, and with a broken constitution, John resolved it should not produce the same effect on him.

But while he was applauding himself for this resolution, the door opened, and the figure appeared at it, beckoning and nodding to him, with a familiarity somewhat terrifying. John now started up, determined to pursue it; but the pursuit was stopped by the weak but shrill cries of his uncle, who was struggling at once with the agonies of death and his housekeeper. The poor woman, anxious for her master's reputation and her own, was trying to put on him a clean shirt and nightcap, and Melmoth, who had just sensation enough to perceive they were taking something from him, continued exclaiming feebly, "They are robbing me—robbing me in my last moments—robbing a dying man. John, won't you assist me—I shall die a beggar; they are taking my last shirt—I shall die a beggar."—And the miser died.

* * * *

A few days after the funeral, the will was opened before proper witnesses, and John was found to be left sole heir to his uncle's property, which, though originally moderate, had, by his grasping habits, and parsimonious life, become very considerable.

As the attorney who read the will concluded, he added, "There are some words here, at the corner of the parchment, which do not appear to be part of the will, as they are neither in the form of a codicil, nor is the signature of the testator affixed to them; but, to the best of my belief, they are in the handwriting of the deceased."

As he spoke he showed the lines to Melmoth, who immediately recognized his uncle's hand (that perpendicular and penurious hand, that seems determined to make the most of the very paper, thriftily abridging every word, and leaving scarce an atom of margin), and read, not without some emotion, the following words: "I enjoin my nephew and heir, John Melmoth, to remove, destroy, or cause to be destroyed, the portrait inscribed J. Melmoth, 1646, hanging in my closet. I also enjoin him to search for a manuscript, which I think he will find in the third and lowest left-hand drawer of the mahogany chest standing under that portrait—it is among some papers of no value, such as manuscript sermons, and pamphlets on the improvement of Ireland, and such stuff; he will distinguish it by its being tied round with a black tape, and the paper being very moldy and discolored. He may read it if he will—I think he had better not. At all events, I adjure him, if there be any power in the adjuration of a dying man, to burn it."

After reading this singular memorandum, the business of the meeting was again resumed; and as old Melmoth's will was very clear and legally worded, all was soon settled, the party dispersed, and John Melmoth was left alone.

* * * *

He resolutely entered the closet, shut the door, and proceeded to search for the manuscript. It was soon found, for the directions of old Melmoth were forcibly written, and strongly remembered. The manuscript, old, tattered, and discolored, was taken from the very drawer in which it was mentioned to be laid. Melmoth's hands felt as cold as those of his dead uncle, when he drew the blotted pages from their nook. He sat down to read—there was a dead silence through the house. Melmoth looked wistfully at the candles, snuffed them, and still thought they looked dim, (perchance he thought they burned blue, but such thought he kept to himself). Certain it is, he often changed his posture, and would have changed his chair, had there been more than one in the apartment.

He sank for a few moments into a fit of gloomy abstraction, till the sound of the clock striking twelve made him start—it was the only sound he had heard for some hours, and the sounds produced by inanimate things, while all living beings around are as dead, have at such an hour an effect indescribably awful. John looked at his manuscript with some reluctance, opened it, paused over the first lines, and as the wind sighed round the desolate apartment, and the rain pattered with a mournful sound against the dismantled window, wished—what did he wish for?—he wished the sound of the wind less dismal, and the dash of the rain less monotonous.—He may be forgiven, it was past midnight, and there was not a human being awake but himself within ten miles when he began to read.

* * * *

The manuscript was discolored, obliterated, and mutilated beyond any that had ever before exercised the patience of a reader. Michaelis himself, scrutinizing into the pretended autograph of St. Mark at Venice, never had a harder time of it.—Melmoth could make out only a sentence here and there. The writer, it appeared, was an Englishman of the name of Stanton, who had traveled abroad shortly after the Restoration. Traveling was not then attended with the facilities which modern improvement has introduced, and scholars and literati, the intelligent, the idle, and the curious, wandered over the Continent for years, like Tom Corvat, though they had the modesty, on their return, to entitle the result of their multiplied observations and labors only "crudities."

Stanton, about the year 1676, was in Spain; he was, like most of the travelers of that age, a man of literature, intelligence, and curiosity, but ignorant of the language of the country, and fighting his way at times from convent to convent, in quest of what was called "Hospitality," that is, obtaining board and lodging on the condition of holding a debate in Latin, on some point theological or metaphysical, with any monk who would become the champion of the strife. Now, as the theology was Catholic, and the metaphysics Aristotelian, Stanton sometimes wished himself at the miserable Posada from whose filth and famine he had been fighting his escape; but though his reverend antagonists always denounced his creed, and comforted themselves, even in defeat, with the assurance that he must be damned, on the double score of his being a heretic and an Englishman, they were obliged to confess that his Latin was good, and his logic unanswerable; and he was allowed, in most cases, to sup and sleep in peace. This was not doomed to be his fate on the night of the 17th August 1677, when he found himself in the plains of Valencia, deserted by a cowardly guide, who had been terrified by the sight of a cross erected as a memorial of a murder, had slipped off his mule unperceived, crossing himself every step he took on his retreat from the heretic, and left Stanton amid the terrors of an approaching storm, and the dangers of an unknown country. The sublime and yet softened beauty of the scenery around, had filled the soul of Stanton with delight, and he enjoyed that delight as Englishmen generally do, silently.

The magnificent remains of two dynasties that had passed away, the ruins of Roman palaces, and of Moorish fortresses, were around and above him—the dark and heavy thunder clouds that advanced slowly, seemed like the shrouds of these specters of departed greatness; they approached, but did not yet overwhelm or conceal them, as if Nature herself was for once awed by the power of man; and far below, the lovely valley of Valencia blushed and burned in all the glory of sunset, like a bride receiving the last glowing kiss of the bridegroom before the approach of night. Stanton gazed around. The difference between the architecture of the Roman and Moorish ruins struck him. Among the former are the remains of a theater, and something like a public place; the latter present only the remains of fortresses, embattled, castellated, and fortified from top to bottom—not a loophole for pleasure to get in by—the loopholes were only for arrows; all denoted military power and despotic subjugation a l'outrance. The contrast might have pleased a philosopher, and he might have indulged in the reflection, that though the ancient Greeks and Romans were savages (as Dr. Johnson says all people who want a press must be, and he says truly), yet they were wonderful savages for their time, for they alone have left traces of their taste for pleasure in the countries they conquered, in their superb theaters, temples (which were also dedicated to pleasure one way or another), and baths, while other conquering bands of savages never left anything behind them but traces of their rage for power. So thought Stanton, as he still saw strongly defined, though darkened by the darkening clouds, the huge skeleton of a Roman amphitheater, its arched and gigantic colonnades now admitting a gleam of light, and now commingling with the purple thunder cloud; and now the solid and heavy mass of a Moorish fortress, no light playing between its impermeable walls—the image of power, dark, isolated, impenetrable. Stanton forgot his cowardly guide, his loneliness, his danger amid an approaching storm and an inhospitable country, where his name and country would shut every door against him, and every peal of thunder would be supposed justified by the daring intrusion of a heretic in the dwelling of an old Christian, as the Spanish Catholics absurdly term themselves, to mark the distinction between them and the baptized Moors.

All this was forgot in contemplating the glorious and awful scenery before him—light struggling with darkness—and darkness menacing a light still more terrible, and announcing its menace in the blue and livid mass of cloud that hovered like a destroying angel in the air, its arrows aimed, but their direction awfully indefinite. But he ceased to forget these local and petty dangers, as the sublimity of romance would term them, when he saw the first flash of the lightning, broad and red as the banners of an insulting army whose motto is Vae victis, shatter to atoms the remains of a Roman tower—the rifted stones rolled down the hill, and fell at the feet of Stanton. He stood appalled, and, awaiting his summons from the Power in whose eye pyramids, palaces, and the worms whose toil has formed them, and the worms who toil out their existence under their shadow or their pressure, are perhaps all alike contemptible, he stood collected, and for a moment felt that defiance of danger which danger itself excites, and we love to encounter it as a physical enemy, to bid it "do its worst," and feel that its worst will perhaps be ultimately its best for us. He stood and saw another flash dart its bright, brief, and malignant glance over the ruins of ancient power, and the luxuriance of recent fertility. Singular contrast! The relics of art forever decaying—the productions of nature forever renewed.— (Alas! for what purpose are they renewed, better than to mock at the perishable monuments which men try in vain to rival them by.) The pyramids themselves must perish, but the grass that grows between their disjointed stones will be renewed from year to year.

Stanton was thinking thus, when all power of thought was suspended, by seeing two persons bearing between them the body of a young, and apparently very lovely girl, who had been struck dead by the lightning. Stanton approached, and heard the voices of the bearers repeating, "There is none who will mourn for her!"

"There is none who will mourn for her!" said other voices, as two more bore in their arms the blasted and blackened figure of what had once been a man, comely and graceful—"there is not *one* to mourn for her now!" They were lovers, and he had been consumed by the flash that had destroyed her, while in the act of endeavoring to defend her. As they were about to remove the bodies, a person approached with a calmness of step and demeanor, as if he were alone unconscious of danger, and incapable of fear; and after looking on them for some time, burst into a laugh so loud, wild, and protracted, that the peasants, starting with as much horror at the sound as at that of the storm, hurried away, bearing the corpses with them. Even Stanton's fears were subdued by his astonishment, and, turning to the stranger, who remained standing on the same spot, he asked the reason of such an outrage on humanity. The stranger, slowly turning round, and disclosing a countenance which—(Here the manuscript was illegible for a few lines), said in English—(A long hiatus followed here, and the next passage that was legible, though it proved to be a continuation of the narrative, was but a fragment.)

* * * *

The terrors of the night rendered Stanton a sturdy and unappeasable applicant; and the shrill voice of the old woman, repeating, "no heretic—no English—Mother of God protect us—avaunt Satan!"—combined with the clatter of the wooden casement (peculiar to the houses in Valencia) which she opened to discharge her volley of anathematization, and shut again as the lightning glanced through the aperture, were unable to repel his importunate request for admittance, in a night whose terrors ought to soften all the miserable petty local passions into one awful feeling of fear for the Power who caused it, and compassion for those who were exposed to it.—But Stanton felt there was something more than national bigotry in the exclamations of the old woman; there was a peculiar and personal horror of the English.—And he was right; but this did not diminish the eagerness of his....

* * * *

The house was handsome and spacious, but the melancholy appearance of desertion....

* * * *

—The benches were by the wall, but there were none to sit there; the tables were spread in what had been the hall, but it seemed as if none had gathered round them for many years—the clock struck audibly, there was no voice of mirth or of occupation to drown its sound; time told his awful lesson to silence alone—the hearths were black with fuel long since consumed—the family portraits looked as if they were the only tenants of the mansion; they seemed to say, from their moldering frames, "there are none to gaze on us;" and the echo of the steps of Stanton and his feeble guide, was the only sound audible between the peals of thunder that rolled still awfully, but more distantly—every peal like the exhausted murmurs of a spent heart. As they passed on, a shriek was heard. Stanton paused, and fearful images of the dangers to which travelers on the Continent are exposed in deserted and remote habitations, came into his mind. "Don't heed it," said the old woman, lighting him on with a miserable lamp—"it is only he....

* * * *

The old woman having now satisfied herself, by ocular demonstration, that her English guest, even if he was the devil, had neither horn, hoof, nor tail, that he could bear the sign of the cross without changing his form, and that, when he spoke, not a puff of sulphur came out of his mouth, began to take courage, and at length commenced her story, which, weary and comfortless as Stanton was,....

* * * *

Every obstacle was now removed; parents and relations at last gave up all opposition, and the young pair were united. Never was there a lovelier—they seemed like angels who had only anticipated by a few years their celestial and eternal union. The marriage was solemnized with much pomp, and a few days after there was a feast in that very wainscoted chamber which you paused to remark was so gloomy. It was that night hung with rich tapestry, representing the exploits of the Cid, particularly that of his burning a few Moors who refused to renounce their accursed religion. They were represented beautifully tortured, writhing and howling, and "Mahomet! Mahomet!" issuing out of their mouths, as they called on him in their burning agonies—you could almost hear them scream. At the upper end of the room, under a splendid estrade, over which was an image of the blessed Virgin, sat Donna Isabella de Cardoza, mother to the bride, and near her Donna Ines, the bride, on rich almohadas; the bridegroom sat opposite to her, and though they never spoke to each other, their eyes, slowly raised, but suddenly withdrawn (those eyes that blushed), told to each other the delicious secret of their happiness. Don Pedro de Cardoza had assembled a large party in honor of his daughter's nuptials; among them was an Englishman of the name of *Melmoth*, a traveler; no one knew who had brought him there. He sat silent like the rest, while the iced waters and the sugared wafers were presented to the company. The night was intensely hot, and the moon glowed like a sun over the ruins of Saguntum; the embroidered blinds flapped heavily, as if the wind made an effort to raise them in vain, and then desisted.

(Another defect in the manuscript occurred here, but it was soon supplied.)

* * * *

The company were dispersed through various alleys of the garden; the bridegroom and bride wandered through one where the delicious perfume of the orange trees mingled itself with that of the myrtles in blow. On their return to the ball, both of them asked, Had the company heard the exquisite sounds that floated through the garden just before they quitted it? No one had heard them. They expressed their surprise. The Englishman had never quitted the hall; it was said he smiled with a most particular and extraordinary expression as the remark was made. His silence had been noticed before, but it was ascribed to his ignorance of the Spanish language, an ignorance that Spaniards are not anxious either to expose or remove by speaking to a stranger. The subject of the music was not again reverted to till the guests were seated at supper, when Donna Ines and her young husband, exchanging a smile of delighted surprise, exclaimed they heard the same delicious sounds floating round them. The guests listened, but no one else could hear it—everyone felt there was something extraordinary in this. Hush! was uttered by every voice almost at the same moment. A dead silence followed—you would think, from their intent looks, that they listened with their very eyes. This deep silence, contrasted with the splendor of the feast, and the light effused from torches held by the domestics, produced a singular effect—it seemed for some moments like an assembly of the dead. The silence was interrupted, though the cause of wonder had not ceased, by the entrance of Father Olavida, the Confessor of Donna Isabella, who had been called away previous to the feast, to administer extreme unction to a dying man in the neighborhood. He was a priest of uncommon sanctity, beloved in the family, and respected in the neighborhood, where he had displayed uncommon taste and talents for exorcism—in fact, this was the good Father's forte, and he piqued himself on it accordingly. The devil never fell into worse hands than Father Olavida's, for when he was so contumacious as to resist Latin, and even the first verses of the Gospel of St. John in Greek, which the good Father never had recourse to but in cases of extreme stubbornness and difficulty— (here Stanton recollected the English story of the Boy of Bilson, and blushed even in Spain for his countrymen)— then he always applied to the Inquisition; and if the devils were ever so obstinate before, they were always seen to fly out of the possessed, just as, in the midst of their cries (no doubt of blasphemy), they were tied to the stake. Some held out even till the flames surrounded them; but even the most stubborn must have been dislodged when the operation was over, for the devil himself could no longer tenant a crisp and glutinous lump of cinders. Thus Father Olavida's fame spread far and wide, and the Cardoza family had made uncommon interest to procure him for a Confessor, and happily succeeded. The ceremony he had just been performing had cast a shade over the good Father's countenance, but it dispersed as he mingled among the guests, and was introduced to them. Room was soon made for him, and he happened accidentally to be seated opposite the Englishman. As the wine was presented to him, Father Olavida (who, as I observed, was a man of singular sanctity) prepared to utter a short internal prayer. He hesitated—trembled—desisted; and, putting down the wine, wiped the drops from his forehead with the sleeve of his habit. Donna Isabella gave a sign to a domestic, and other wine of a higher quality was offered to him. His lips moved, as if in the effort to pronounce a benediction on it and the company, but the effort again failed; and the change in his countenance was so extraordinary, that it was perceived by all the guests. He felt the sensation that his extraordinary appearance excited, and attempted to remove it by again endeavoring to lift the cup to his lips. So strong was the anxiety with which the company watched him, that the only sound heard in that spacious and crowded hall was the rustling of his habit as he attempted to lift the cup to his lips once more—in vain. The guests sat in astonished silence. Father Olavida alone remained standing; but at that moment the Englishman rose, and appeared determined to fix Olavida's regards by a gaze like that of fascination. Olavida rocked, reeled, grasped the arm of a page, and at last, closing his eyes for a moment, as if to escape the horrible fascination of that unearthly glare (the Englishman's eyes were observed by all the guests, from the moment of his entrance, to effuse a most fearful and preternatural luster), exclaimed, "Who is among us?—Who?—I cannot utter a blessing while he is here. I cannot feel one. Where he treads, the earth is parched!—Where he breathes, the air is fire!—Where he feeds, the food is poison!—Where he turns his glance is lightning!—*Who is among us?—Who?*" repeated the priest in the agony of adjuration, while his cowl fallen back, his few thin hairs around the scalp instinct and alive with terrible emotion, his outspread arms protruded from the sleeves of his habit, and extended toward the awful stranger, suggested the idea of an inspired being in the dreadful rapture of prophetic denunciation. He stood— still stood, and the Englishman stood calmly opposite to him. There was an agitated irregularity in the attitudes of those around them, which contrasted strongly the fixed and stern postures of those two, who remained gazing silently at each other. "Who knows him?" exclaimed Olavida, starting apparently from a trance; "who knows him? who brought him here?"

The guests severally disclaimed all knowledge of the Englishman, and each asked the other in whispers, "who *had* brought him there?" Father Olavida then pointed his arm to each of the company, and asked each individually, "Do you know him?" No! no! no!" was uttered with vehement emphasis by every individual. "But I know him," said Olavida, "by these cold drops!" and he wiped them off—"by these convulsed joints!" and he attempted to sign the cross, but could not. He raised his voice, and evidently speaking with increased difficulty—"By this bread and wine, which the faithful receive as the body and blood of Christ, but which *his* presence converts into matter as viperous as the suicide foam of the dying Judas—by all these—I know him, and command him to be gone!—He is—he is—" and he bent forward as he spoke, and gazed on the Englishman with an expression which the mixture of rage, hatred, and fear rendered terrible. All the guests rose at these words—the whole company now presented two singular groups, that of the amazed guests all collected together, and repeating, "Who, what is he?" and that of the Englishman, who stood unmoved, and Olavida, who dropped dead in the attitude of pointing to him.

* * * *

The body was removed into another room, and the departure of the Englishman was not noticed till the company returned to the hall. They sat late together, conversing on this extraordinary circumstance, and finally agreed to remain in the house, lest the evil spirit (for they believed the Englishman no better) should take certain liberties with the corse by no means agreeable to a Catholic, particularly as he had manifestly died without the benefit of the last sacraments. Just as this laudable resolution was formed, they were roused by cries of horror and agony from the bridal chamber, where the young pair had retired.

They hurried to the door, but the father was first. They burst it open, and found the bride a corse in the arms of her husband.

* * * *

He never recovered his reason; the family deserted the mansion rendered terrible by so many misfortunes. One apartment is still tenanted by the unhappy maniac; his were the cries you heard as you traversed the deserted rooms. He is for the most part silent during the day, but at midnight he always exclaims, in a voice frightfully piercing, and hardly human, "They are coming! they are coming!" and relapses into profound silence.

The funeral of Father Olavida was attended by an extraordinary circumstance. He was interred in a neighboring convent; and the reputation of his sanctity, joined to the interest caused by his extraordinary death, collected vast numbers at the ceremony. His funeral sermon was preached by a monk of distinguished eloquence, appointed for the purpose. To render the effect of his discourse more powerful, the corse, extended on a bier, with its face uncovered, was placed in the aisle. The monk took his text from one of the prophets—"Death is gone up into our palaces." He expatiated on mortality, whose approach, whether abrupt or lingering, is alike awful to man.—He spoke of the vicisstudes of empires with much eloquence and learning, but his audience were not observed to be much affected.—He cited various passages from the lives of the saints, descriptive of the glories of martyrdom, and the heroism of those who had bled and blazed for Christ and his blessed mother, but they appeared still waiting for something to touch them more deeply. When he inveighed against the tyrants under whose bloody persecution those holy men suffered, his hearers were roused for a moment, for it is always easier to excite a passion than a moral feeling. But when he spoke of the dead, and pointed with emphatic gesture to the corse, as it lay before them cold and motionless, every eye was fixed, and every ear became attentive. Even the lovers, who, under pretense of dipping their fingers into the holy water, were contriving to exchange amorous billets, forbore for one moment this interesting intercourse, to listen to the preacher. He dwelt with much energy on the virtues of the deceased, whom he declared to be a particular favorite of the Virgin; and enumerating the various losses that would be caused by his departure to the community to which he belonged, to society, and to religion at large; he at last worked up himself to a vehement expostulation with the Deity on the occasion. "Why hast thou," he exclaimed, "why hast thou, Oh God! thus dealt with us? Why hast thou snatched from our sight this glorious saint, whose merits, if properly applied, doubtless would have been sufficient to atone for the apostasy of St. Peter, the opposition of St. Paul (previous to his conversion), and even the treachery of Judas himself? Why hast thou, Oh God! snatched him from us?"—and a deep and hollow voice from among the congregation answered—"Because he deserved his fate." The murmurs of approbation with which the congregation honored this apostrophe half drowned this extraordinary interruption; and though there was some little commotion in the immediate vicinity of the speaker, the rest of the audience continued to listen intently. "What," proceeded the preacher, pointing to the corse, "what hath laid thee there, servant of God?"—"Pride, ignorance, and fear," answered the same voice, in accents still more thrilling. The disturbance now became universal. The preacher paused, and a circle opening, disclosed the figure of a monk belonging to the convent, who stood among them.

* * * *

After all the usual modes of admonition, exhortation, and discipline had been employed, and the bishop of the diocese, who, under the report of these extraordinary circumstances, had visited the convent in person to obtain some explanation from the contumacious monk in vain, it was agreed, in a chapter extraordinary, to surrender him to the power of the Inquisition. He testified great horror when this determination was made known to him—and offered to tell over and over again all that he *could* relate of the cause of Father Olavida's death. His humiliation, and repeated offers of confession, came too late. He was conveyed to the Inquisition. The proceedings of that tribunal are rarely disclosed, but there is a secret report (I cannot answer for its truth) of what he said and suffered there. On his first examination, he said he would relate all he *could*. He was told that was not enough, he must relate all he knew.

* * * *

"Why did you testify such horror at the funeral of Father Olavida?"—"Everyone testified horror and grief at the death of that venerable ecclesiastic, who died in the odor of sanctity. Had I done otherwise, it might have been reckoned a proof of my guilt." "Why did you interrupt the preacher with such extraordinary exclamations?"—To this no answer. "Why do you refuse to explain the meaning of those exclamations?"—No answer. "Why do you persist in this obstinate and dangerous silence? Look, I beseech you, brother, at the cross that is suspended against this wall," and the Inquisitor pointed to the large black crucifix at the back of the chair where he sat; "one drop of the blood shed there can purify you from all the sin you have ever committed; but all that blood, combined with the intercession of the Queen of Heaven, and the merits of all its martyrs, nay, even the absolution of the Pope, cannot deliver you from the curse of dying in unrepented sin."—"What sin, then, have I committed?"—"The greatest of all possible sins; you refuse answering the questions put to you at the tribunal of the most holy and merciful Inquisition—you will not tell us what you know concerning the death of Father Olavida."—"I have told you that I believe he perished in consequence of his ignorance and presumption." "What proof can you produce of that?"—"He sought the knowledge of a secret withheld from man." "What was that?"—"The secret of discovering the presence or agency of the evil power." "Do you possess that secret?"—After much agitation on the part of the prisoner, he said distinctly, but very faintly, "My master forbids me to disclose it." "If your master were Jesus Christ, he would not forbid you to obey the commands, or answer the questions of the Inquisition."—"I am not sure of that." There was a general outcry of horror at these words. The examination then went on. "If you believed Olavida to be guilty of any pursuits or studies condemned by our mother the church, why did you not denounce him to the Inquisition?"—"Because I believed him not likely to be injured by such pursuits; his mind was too weak—he died in the struggle," said the prisoner with great emphasis. "You believe, then, it requires strength of mind to keep those abominable secrets, when examined as to their nature and tendency?"—"No, I rather imagine strength of body." "We shall try that presently," said an Inquisitor, giving a signal for the torture.

* * * *

The prisoner underwent the first and second applications with unshrinking courage, but on the infliction of the water-torture, which is indeed insupportable to humanity, either to suffer or relate, he exclaimed in the gasping interval, he would disclose everything. He was released, refreshed, restored, and the following day uttered the following remarkable confession....

* * * *

The old Spanish woman further confessed to Stanton, that....

* * * *

and that the Englishman certainly had been seen in the neighborhood since—seen, as she had heard, that very night. "Great G—d!" exclaimed Stanton, as he recollected the stranger whose demoniac laugh had so appalled him, while gazing on the lifeless bodies of the lovers, whom the lightning had struck and blasted.

As the manuscript, after a few blotted and illegible pages, became more distinct, Melmoth read on, perplexed and unsatisfied, not knowing what connection this Spanish story could have with his ancestor, whom, however, he recognized under the title of the Englishman; and wondering how Stanton could have thought it worth his while to follow him to Ireland, write a long manuscript about an event that occurred in Spain, and leave it in the hands of his family, to "verify untrue things," in the language of Dogberry—his wonder was diminished, though his curiosity was still more inflamed, by the perusal of the next lines, which he made out with some difficulty. It seems Stanton was now in England.

* * * *

About the year 1677, Stanton was in London, his mind still full of his mysterious countryman. This constant subject of his contemplations had produced a visible change in his exterior—his walk was what Sallust tells us of Catiline's—his were, too, the "faedi oculi." He said to himself every moment, "If I could but trace that being, I will not call him man,"—and the next moment he said, "and what if I could?" In this state of mind, it is singular enough that he mixed constantly in public amusements, but it is true. When one fierce passion is devouring the soul, we feel more than ever the necessity of external excitement; and our dependence on the world for temporary relief increases in direct proportion to our contempt of the world and all its works. He went frequently to the theaters, *then* fashionable, when

"*The fair sat panting at a courtier's play,*
And not a mask went unimproved away."

* * * *

It was that memorable night, when, according to the history of the veteran Betterton,* Mrs. Barry, who personated Roxana, had a green- room squabble with Mrs. Bowtell, the representative of Statira, about a veil, which the partiality of the property man adjudged to the latter. Roxana suppressed her rage till the fifth act, when, stabbing Statira, she aimed the blow with such force as to pierce through her stays, and inflict a severe though not dangerous wound. Mrs. Bowtell fainted, the performance was suspended, and, in the commotion which this incident caused in the house, many of the audience rose, and Stanton among them. It was at this moment that, in a seat opposite to him, he discovered the object of his search for four years—the Englishman whom he had met in the plains of Valencia, and whom he believed the same with the subject of the extraordinary narrative he had heard there.

* Vide Betterton's History of the Stage.

He was standing up. There was nothing particular or remarkable in his appearance, but the expression of his eyes could never be mistaken or forgotten. The heart of Stanton palpitated with violence—a mist overspread his eye—a nameless and deadly sickness, accompanied with a creeping sensation in every pore, from which cold drops were gushing, announced the....

* * * *

Before he had well recovered, a strain of music, soft, solemn, and delicious, breathed round him, audibly ascending from the ground, and increasing in sweetness and power till it seemed to fill the whole building. Under the sudden impulse of amazement and pleasure, he inquired of some around him from whence those exquisite sounds arose. But, by the manner in which he was answered, it was plain that those he addressed considered him insane; and, indeed, the remarkable change in his expression might well justify the suspicion. He then remembered that night in Spain, when the same sweet and mysterious sounds were heard only by the young bridegroom and bride, of whom the latter perished on that very night. "And am I then to be the next victim?" thought Stanton; "and are those celestial sounds, that seem to prepare us for heaven, only intended to announce the presence of an incarnate fiend, who mocks the devoted with 'airs from heaven,' while he prepares to surround them with 'blasts from hell'?" It is very singular that at this moment, when his imagination had reached its highest pitch of elevation—when the object he had pursued so long and fruitlessly, had in one moment become as it were tangible to the grasp both of mind and body—when this spirit, with whom he had wrestled in darkness, was at last about to declare its name, that Stanton began to feel a kind of disappointment at the futility of his pursuits, like Bruce at discovering the source of the Nile, or Gibbon on concluding his History. The feeling which he had dwelt on so long, that he had actually converted it into a duty, was after all mere curiosity; but what passion is more insatiable, or more capable of giving a kind of romantic grandeur to all its wanderings and eccentricities? Curiosity is in one respect like love, it always compromises between the object and the feeling; and provided the latter possesses sufficient energy, no matter how contemptible the former may be. A child might have smiled at the agitation of Stanton, caused as it was by the accidental appearance of a stranger; but no man, in the full energy of his passions, was there, but must have trembled at the horrible agony of emotion with which he felt approaching, with sudden and irresistible velocity, the crisis of his destiny.

When the play was over, he stood for some moments in the deserted streets. It was a beautiful moonlight night, and he saw near him a figure, whose shadow, projected half across the street (there were no flagged ways then, chains and posts were the only defense of the foot passenger), appeared to him of gigantic magnitude. He had been so long accustomed to contend with these phantoms of the imagination, that he took a kind of stubborn delight in subduing them. He walked up to the object, and observing the shadow only was magnified, and the figure was the ordinary height of man, he approached it, and discovered the very object of his search—the man whom he had seen for a moment in Valencia, and, after a search of four years, recognized at the theater.

* * * *

"You were in quest of me?"—"I was." "Have you anything to inquire of me?"—"Much." "Speak, then."—"This is no place." "No place! poor wretch, I am independent of time and place. Speak, if you have anything to ask or to learn."—"I have many things to ask, but nothing to learn, I hope, from you." "You deceive yourself, but you will be undeceived when next we meet."—"And when shall that be?" said Stanton, grasping his arm; "name your hour and your place."

"The hour shall be midday," answered the stranger, with a horrid and unintelligible smile; "and the place shall be the bare walls of a madhouse, where you shall rise rattling in your chains, and rustling from your straw, to greet me—yet still you shall have *the curse of sanity*, and of memory. My voice shall ring in your ears till then, and the glance of these eyes shall be reflected from every object, animate or inanimate, till you behold them again."—"Is it under circumstances so horrible we are to meet again?" said Stanton, shrinking under the full-lighted blaze of those demon eyes. "I never," said the stranger, in an emphatic tone—"I never desert my friends in misfortune. When they are plunged in the lowest abyss of human calamity, they are sure to be visited by me."

* * * *

The narrative, when Melmoth was again able to trace its continuation, described Stanton, some years after, plunged in a state the most deplorable.

He had been always reckoned of a singular turn of mind, and the belief of this, aggravated by his constant talk of Melmoth, his wild pursuit of him, his strange behavior at the theater, and his dwelling on the various particulars of their extraordinary meetings, with all the intensity of the deepest conviction (while he never could impress them on any one's conviction but his own), suggested to some prudent people the idea that he was deranged. Their malignity probably took part with their prudence. The selfish Frenchman* says, we feel a pleasure even in the misfortunes of our friends—a plus forte in those of our enemies; and as everyone is an enemy to a man of genius of course, the report of Stanton's malady was propagated with infernal and successful industry. Stanton's next relative, a needy unprincipled man, watched the report in its circulation, and saw the snares closing round his victim. He waited on him one morning, accompanied by a person of a grave, though somewhat repulsive appearance. Stanton was as usual abstracted and restless, and, after a few moments' conversation, he proposed a drive a few miles out of London, which he said would revive and refresh him. Stanton objected, on account of the difficulty of getting a hackney coach (for it is singular that at this period the number of private equipages, though infinitely fewer than they are now, exceeded the number of hired ones), and proposed going by water. This, however, did not suit the kinsman's views; and, after pretending to send for a carriage (which was in waiting at the end of the street), Stanton and his companions entered it, and drove about two miles out of London.

* Rochefoucauld.

The carriage then stopped. Come, Cousin," said the younger Stanton—"come and view a purchase I have made." Stanton absently alighted, and followed him across a small paved court; the other person followed. "In troth, Cousin," said Stanton, "your choice appears not to have been discreetly made; your house has somewhat of a gloomy aspect."—"Hold you content, Cousin," replied the other; "I shall take order that you like it better, when you have been some time a dweller therein." Some attendants of a mean appearance, and with most suspicious visages, awaited them on their entrance, and they ascended a narrow staircase, which led to a room meanly furnished. "Wait here," said the kinsman, to the man who accompanied them, "till I go for company to divertise my cousin in his loneliness." They were left alone. Stanton took no notice of his companion, but as usual seized the first book near him, and began to read. It was a volume in manuscript—they were then much more common than now.

The first lines struck him as indicating insanity in the writer. It was a wild proposal (written apparently after the great fire of London) to rebuild it with stone, and attempting to prove, on a calculation wild, false, and yet sometimes plausible, that this could be done out of the colossal fragments of Stonehenge, which the writer proposed to remove for that purpose. Subjoined were several grotesque drawings of engines designed to remove those massive blocks, and in a corner of the page was a note—"I would have drawn these more accurately, but was not allowed a *knife* to mend my pen."

The next was entitled, "A modest proposal for the spreading of Christianity in foreign parts, whereby it is hoped its entertainment will become general all over the world."—This modest proposal was, to convert the Turkish ambassadors (who had been in London a few years before), by offering them their choice of being strangled on the spot, or becoming Christians. Of course the writer reckoned on their embracing the easier alternative, but even this was to be clogged with a heavy condition—namely, that they must be bound before a magistrate to convert twenty Mussulmans a day, on their return to Turkey. The rest of the pamphlet was reasoned very much in the conclusive style of Captain Bobadil—these twenty will convert twenty more apiece, and these two hundred converts, converting their due number in the same time, all Turkey would be converted before the Grand Signior knew where he was. Then comes the coup d'eclat—one fine morning, every minaret in Constantinople was to ring out with bells, instead of the cry of the Muezzins; and the

Imaum, coming out to see what was the matter, was to be encountered by the Archbishop of Canterbury, in pontificalibus, performing Cathedral service in the church of St. Sophia, which was to finish the business. Here an objection appeared to arise, which the ingenuity of the writer had anticipated.—"It may be redargued," saith he, "by those who have more spleen than brain, that forasmuch as the Archbishop preacheth in English, he will not thereby much edify the Turkish folk, who do altogether hold in a vain gabble of their own." But this (to use his own language) he "evites," by judiciously observing, that where service was performed in an unknown tongue, the devotion of the people was always observed to be much increased thereby; as, for instance, in the church of Rome—that St. Augustine, with his monks, advanced to meet King Ethelbert singing litanies (in a language his majesty could not possibly have understood), and converted him and his whole court on the spot—that the sybilline books....

* * * *

Cum multis aliis.

Between the pages were cut most exquisitely in paper the likenesses of some of these Turkish ambassadors; the hair of the beards, in particular, was feathered with a delicacy of touch that seemed the work of fairy fingers—but the pages ended with a complaint of the operator, that his scissors had been taken from him. However, he consoled himself and the reader with the assurance, that he would that night catch a moonbeam as it entered through the grating, and, when he had whetted it on the iron knobs of his door, would do wonders with it. In the next page was found a melancholy proof of powerful but prostrated intellect. It contained some insane lines, ascribed to Lee the dramatic poet, commencing,

"O that my lungs could bleat like buttered pease," &c.

There is no proof whatever that these miserable lines were really written by Lee, except that the measure is the fashionable quatrain of the period. It is singular that Stanton read on without suspicion of his own danger, quite absorbed in the album of a madhouse, without ever reflecting on the place where he was, and which such compositions too manifestly designated.

It was after a long interval that he looked round, and perceived that his companion was gone. Bells were unusual then. He proceeded to the door—it was fastened. He called aloud—his voice was echoed in a moment by many others, but in tones so wild and discordant, that he desisted in involuntary terror. As the day advanced, and no one approached, he tried the window, and then perceived for the first time it was grated. It looked out on the narrow flagged yard, in which no human being was; and if there had, from such a being no human feeling could have been extracted.

Sickening with unspeakable horror, he sunk rather than sat down beside the miserable window, and "wished for day."

* * * *

At midnight he started from a doze, half a swoon, half a sleep, which probably the hardness of his seat, and of the deal table on which he leaned, had not contributed to prolong.

He was in complete darkness; the horror of his situation struck him at once, and for a moment he was indeed almost qualified for an inmate of that dreadful mansion.

He felt his way to the door, shook it with desperate strength, and uttered the most frightful cries, mixed with expostulations and commands. His cries were in a moment echoed by a hundred voices. In maniacs there is a peculiar malignity, accompanied by an extraordinary acuteness of some of the senses, particularly in distinguishing the voice of a stranger. The cries that he heard on every side seemed like a wild and infernal yell of joy, that their mansion of misery had obtained another tenant.

He paused, exhausted—a quick and thundering step was heard in the passage. The door was opened, and a man of savage appearance stood at the entrance—two more were seen indistinctly in the passage. "Release me, villain!"—"Stop, my fine fellow, what's all this noise for?" "Where am I?" "Where you ought to be." "Will you dare to detain me?"—"Yes, and a little more than that," answered the ruffian, applying a loaded horsewhip to his back and shoulders, till the patient soon fell to the ground convulsed with rage and pain. "Now you see you are where you ought to be," repeated the ruffian, brandishing the horsewhip over him, "and now take the advice of a friend, and make no more noise. The lads are ready for you with the darbies, and they'll clink them on in the crack of this whip, unless you prefer another touch of it first." They then were advancing into the room as he spoke, with fetters in their hands (strait waistcoats being then little known or used), and showed, by their frightful countenances and gestures, no unwillingness to apply them. Their harsh rattle on the stone pavement made Stanton's blood run cold; the effect, however, was useful. He had the presence of mind to acknowledge his (supposed) miserable condition, to supplicate the forbearance of the ruthless keeper, and promise complete submission to his orders. This pacified the ruffian, and he retired.

Stanton collected all his resolution to encounter the horrible night; he saw all that was before him, and summoned himself to meet it. After much agitated deliberation, he conceived it best to continue the same appearance of submission and tranquillity, hoping that thus he might in time either propitiate the wretches in whose hands he was, or, by his apparent inoffensiveness, procure such opportunities of indulgence, as might perhaps ultimately facilitate his escape. He therefore determined to conduct himself with the utmost tranquillity, and never to let his voice be heard in the house; and he laid down several other resolutions with a degree of prudence which he already shuddered to think might be the cunning of incipient madness, or the beginning result of the horrid habits of the place.

These resolutions were put to desperate trial that very night. Just next to Stanton's apartment were lodged two most uncongenial neighbors. One of them was a puritanical weaver, who had been driven mad by a single sermon from the celebrated Hugh Peters, and was sent to the madhouse as full of election and reprobation as he could hold—and fuller. He regularly repeated over the five points while daylight lasted, and imagined himself preaching in a conventicle with distinguished success; toward twilight his visions were more gloomy, and at midnight his blasphemies became horrible. In the opposite cell was lodged a loyalist tailor, who had been ruined by giving credit to the cavaliers and their ladies—(for at this time, and much later, down to the reign of Anne, tailors were employed by females even to make and fit on their stays)—who had run mad with drink and loyalty on the burning of the Rump, and ever since had made the cells of the madhouse echo with fragments of the ill-fated Colonel Lovelace's song, scraps from Cowley's "Cutter of Coleman street," and some curious specimens from Mrs. Aphra Behn's plays, where the cavaliers are denominated the heroicks, and Lady Lambert and Lady Desborough represented as going to meeting, their large Bibles carried before them by their pages, and falling in love with two banished cavaliers by the way. The voice in which he shrieked out such words was powerfully horrible, but it was like the moan of an infant compared to the voice which took up and reechoed the cry, in a tone that made the building shake. It was the voice of a maniac, who had lost her husband, children, subsistence, and finally her reason, in the dreadful fire of London. The cry of fire never failed to operate with terrible punctuality on her associations. She had been in a disturbed sleep, and now started from it as suddenly as on that dreadful night. It was Saturday night too, and she was always observed to be particularly violent on that night—it was the terrible weekly festival of insanity with her. She was awake, and busy in a moment escaping from the flames; and she dramatized the whole scene with such hideous fidelity, that Stanton's resolution was far more in danger from her than from the battle between his neighbors Testimony and Hothead. She began exclaiming she was suffocated by the smoke; then she sprung from her bed, calling for a light, and appeared to be struck by the sudden glare that burst through her casement.—"The last day," she shrieked, "The last day! The very heavens are on fire!"—"That will not come till the Man of Sin be first destroyed," cried the weaver; "thou ravest of light and fire, and yet thou art in utter darkness.—I pity thee, poor mad soul, I pity thee!" The maniac never heeded him; she appeared to be scrambling up a staircase to her children's room. She exclaimed she was scorched, singed, suffocated; her courage appeared to fail, and she retreated. "But my children are there!" she cried in a voice of unspeakable agony, as she seemed to make another effort; "here I am—here I am come to save you.—Oh God! They are all blazing!—Take this arm—no, not that, it is scorched and disabled—well, any arm—take hold of my clothes—no, they are blazing too!—Well, take me all on fire as I am!—And their hair, how it hisses!—Water, one drop of water for my youngest—he is but an infant—for my youngest, and let me burn!" She paused in horrid silence, to watch the fall of a blazing rafter that was about to shatter the staircase on which she stood.—"The roof has fallen on my head!" she exclaimed. "The earth is weak, and all the inhabitants thereof," chanted the weaver; "I bear up the pillars of it."

The maniac marked the destruction of the spot where she thought she stood by one desperate bound, accompanied by a wild shriek, and then calmly gazed on her infants as they rolled over the scorching fragments, and sunk into the abyss of fire below. "There they go—one—two—three—all!" and her voice sunk into low mutterings, and her convulsions into faint, cold shudderings, like the sobbings of a spent storm, as she imagined herself to "stand in safety and despair," amid the thousand houseless wretches assembled in the suburbs of London on the dreadful nights after the fire, without food, roof, or raiment, all gazing on the burning ruins of their dwellings and their property. She seemed to listen to their complaints, and even repeated some of them very affectingly, but invariably answered them with the same words, "But

I have lost all my children—all!" It was remarkable, that when this sufferer began to rave, all the others became silent. The cry of nature hushed every other cry—she was the only patient in the house who was not mad from politics, religion, ebriety, or some perverted passion; and terrifying as the outbreak of her frenzy always was, Stanton used to await it as a kind of relief from the dissonant, melancholy, and ludicrous ravings of the others.

But the utmost efforts of his resolution began to sink under the continued horrors of the place. The impression on his senses began to defy the power of reason to resist them. He could not shut out these frightful cries nightly repeated, nor the frightful sound of the whip employed to still them. Hope began to fail him, as he observed, that the submissive tranquillity (which he had imagined, by obtaining increased indulgence, might contribute to his escape, or perhaps convince the keeper of his sanity) was interpreted by the callous ruffian, who was acquainted only with the varieties of *madness*, as a more refined species of that cunning which he was well accustomed to watch and baffle.

On his first discovery of his situation, he had determined to take the utmost care of his health and intellect that the place allowed, as the sole basis of his hope of deliverance. But as that hope declined, he neglected the means of realizing it. He had at first risen early, walked incessantly about his cell, and availed himself of every opportunity of being in the open air. He took the strictest care of his person in point of cleanliness, and with or without appetite, regularly forced down his miserable meals; and all these efforts were even pleasant, as long as hope prompted them. But now he began to relax them all. He passed half the day in his wretched bed, in which he frequently took his meals, declined shaving or changing his linen, and, when the sun shone into his cell, he turned from it on his straw with a sigh of heartbroken despondency. Formerly, when the air breathed through his grating, he used to say, "Blessed air of heaven, I shall breathe you once more in freedom!—Reserve all your freshness for that delicious evening when I shall inhale you, and be as free as you myself." Now when he felt it, he sighed and said nothing. The twitter of the sparrows, the pattering of rain, or the moan of the wind, sounds that he used to sit up in his bed to catch with delight, as reminding him of nature, were now unheeded.

He began at times to listen with sullen and horrible pleasure to the cries of his miserable companions. He became squalid, listless, torpid, and disgusting in his appearance.

* * * *

It was one of those dismal nights, that, as he tossed on his loathsome bed—more loathsome from the impossibility to quit it without feeling more "unrest,"—he perceived the miserable light that burned in the hearth was obscured by the intervention of some dark object. He turned feebly toward the light, without curiosity, without excitement, but with a wish to diversify the monotony of his misery, by observing the slightest change made even accidentally in the dusky atmosphere of his cell. Between him and the light stood the figure of Melmoth, just as he had seen him from the first; the figure was the same; the expression of the face was the same—cold, stony, and rigid; the eyes, with their infernal and dazzling luster, were still the same.

Stanton's ruling passion rushed on his soul; he felt this apparition like a summons to a high and fearful encounter. He heard his heart beat audibly, and could have exclaimed with Lee's unfortunate heroine—"It pants as cowards do before a battle; Oh the great march has sounded!"

Melmoth approached him with that frightful calmness that mocks the terror it excites. "My prophecy has been fulfilled—you rise to meet me rattling from your chains, and rustling from your straw—am I not a true prophet?" Stanton was silent. "Is not your situation very miserable?"—Still Stanton was silent; for he was beginning to believe this an illusion of madness. He thought to himself, "How could he have gained entrance here?"— "Would you not wish to be delivered from it?" Stanton tossed on his straw, and its rustling seemed to answer the question. "I have the power to deliver you from it." Melmoth spoke very slowly and very softly, and the melodious smoothness of his voice made a frightful contrast to the stony rigor of his features, and the fiendlike brilliancy of his eyes. "Who are you, and whence come you?" said Stanton, in a tone that was meant to be interrogatory and imperative, but which, from his habits of squalid debility, was at once feeble and querulous. His intellect had become affected by the gloom of his miserable habitation, as the wretched inmate of a similar mansion, when produced before a medical examiner, was reported to be a complete Albino.—His skin was bleached, his eyes turned white; he could not bear the light; and, when exposed to it, he turned away with a mixture of weakness and restlessness, more like the writhings of a sick infant than the struggles of a man.

Such was Stanton's situation. He was enfeebled now, and the power of the enemy seemed without a possibility of opposition from either his intellectual or corporeal powers.

* * * *

Of all their horrible dialogue, only these words were legible in the manuscript, "You know me now."—"I always knew you."—"That is false; you imagined you did, and that has been the cause of all the wild ... of the ...... of your finally being lodged in this mansion of misery, where only I would seek, where only I can succor you."—"You, demon!"—"Demon!—Harsh words!—Was it a demon or a human being placed you here?—Listen to me, Stanton; nay, wrap not yourself in that miserable blanket—that cannot shut out my words. Believe me, were you folded in thunder clouds, you must hear *me*! Stanton, think of your misery. These bare walls—what do they present to the intellect or to the senses?—Whitewash, diversified with the scrawls of charcoal or red chalk, that your happy predecessors have left for you to trace over. You have a taste for drawing—I trust it will improve. And here's a grating, through which the sun squints on you like a stepdame, and the breeze blows, as if it meant to tantalize you with a sigh from that sweet mouth, whose kiss you must never enjoy. And where's your library—intellectual man—traveled man?" he repeated in a tone of bitter derision; "where be your companions, your peaked men of countries, as your favorite Shakespeare has it? You must be content with the spider and the rat, to crawl and scratch round your flock bed! I have known prisoners in the Bastille to feed them for companions—why don't you begin your task? I have known a spider to descend at the tap of a finger, and a rat to come forth when the daily meal was brought, to share it with his fellow prisoner!—How delightful to have vermin for your guests! Aye, and when the feast fails them, they make a meal of their entertainer!—You shudder.—Are you, then, the first prisoner who has been devoured alive by the vermin that infested his cell?—Delightful banquet, not 'where you eat, but where you are eaten'! Your guests, however, will give you one token of repentance while they feed; there will be gnashing of teeth, and you shall hear it, and feel it too perchance!—And then for meals—Oh you are daintily off!—The soup that the cat has lapped; and (as her progeny has probably contributed to the hell broth) why not? Then your hours of solitude, deliciously diversified by the yell of famine, the howl of madness, the crash of whips, and the broken-hearted sob of those who, like you, are supposed, or *driven* mad by the crimes of others!—Stanton, do you imagine your reason can possibly hold out amid such scenes?—Supposing your reason was unimpaired, your health not destroyed—suppose all this, which is, after all, more than fair supposition can grant, guess the effect of the continuance of these scenes on your senses alone. A time will come, and soon, when, from mere habit, you will echo the scream of every delirious wretch that harbors near you; then you will pause, clasp your hands on your throbbing head, and listen with horrible anxiety whether the scream proceeded from *you* or *them*. The time will come, when, from the want of occupation, the listless and horrible vacancy of your hours, you will feel as anxious to hear those shrieks, as you were at first terrified to hear them—when you will watch for the ravings of your next neighbor, as you would for a scene on the stage. All humanity will be extinguished in you. The ravings of these wretches will become at once your sport and your torture. You will watch for the sounds, to mock them with the grimaces and bellowings of a fiend. The mind has a power of accommodating itself to its situation, that you will experience in its most frightful and deplorable efficacy. Then comes the dreadful doubt of one's own sanity, the terrible announcer that *that* doubt will soon become fear, and *that* fear certainty. Perhaps (still more dreadful) the *fear* will at last become a *hope*—shut out from society, waMtched by a brutal keeper, writhing with all the impotent agony of an incarcerated mind, without communication and without sympathy, unable to exchange ideas but with those whose ideas are only the hideous specters of departed intellect, or even to hear the welcome sound of the human voice, except to mistake it for the howl of a fiend, and stop the ear desecrated by its intrusion—then at last your fear will become a more fearful hope; you will wish to become one of them, to escape the agony of consciousness. As those who have long leaned over a precipice, have at last felt a desire to plunge below, to relieve the intolerable temptation of their giddiness,* you will hear them laugh amid their wildest paroxysms; you will say, 'Doubtless those wretches have some consolation, but I have none; my sanity is my greatest curse in this abode of horrors. They greedily devour their miserable meals, while I loathe mine. They sleep sometimes soundly, while my sleep is—worse than their waking. They are revived every morning by some delicious illusion of cunning madness, soothing them with the hope of escaping, baffling or tormenting their keeper; my sanity precludes all such hope. *I know I never can escape*, and the preservation of my faculties is only an aggravation of my sufferings.

I have all their miseries—I have none of their consolations. They laugh—I hear them; would I could laugh like them.' You will try, and the very effort will be an invocation to the demon of insanity to come and take full possession of you from that moment forever."

* A fact, related to me by a person who was near committing suicide in a similar situation, to escape what he called "the excruciating torture of giddiness."

(There were other details, both of the menaces and temptations employed by Melmoth, which are too horrible for insertion. One of them may serve for an instance.)

"You think that the intellectual power is something distinct from the vitality of the soul, or, in other words, that if even your reason should be destroyed (which it nearly is), your soul might yet enjoy beatitude in the full exercise of its enlarged and exalted faculties, and all the clouds which obscured them be dispelled by the Sun of Righteousness, in whose beams you hope to bask forever and ever. Now, without going into any metaphysical subtleties about the distinction between mind and soul, experience must teach you, that there can be no crime into which madmen would not, and do not, precipitate themselves; mischief is their occupation, malice their habit, murder their sport, and blasphemy their delight. Whether a soul in this state can be in a hopeful one, it is for you to judge; but it seems to me, that with the loss of reason (and reason cannot long be retained in this place) you lose also the hope of immortality.—Listen," said the tempter, pausing, "listen to the wretch who is raving near you, and whose blasphemies might make a demon start.—He was once an eminent puritanical preacher. Half the day he imagines himself in a pulpit, denouncing damnation against Papists, Arminians, and even Sublapsarians (he being a Supra-lapsarian himself). He foams, he writhes, he gnashes his teeth; you would imagine him in the hell he was painting, and that the fire and brimstone he is so lavish of were actually exhaling from his jaws. At night his creed retaliates on him; he believes himself one of the reprobates he has been all day denouncing, and curses God for the very decree he has all day been glorifying Him for.

"He, whom he has for twelve hours been vociferating 'is the loveliest among ten thousand,' becomes the object of demoniac hostility and execration. He grapples with the iron posts of his bed, and says he is rooting out the cross from the very foundations of Calvary; and it is remarkable, that in proportion as his morning exercises are intense, vivid, and eloquent, his nightly blasphemies are outrageous and horrible.—Hark! Now he believes himself a demon; listen to his diabolical eloquence of horror!"

Stanton listened, and shuddered…

* * * *

"Escape—escape for your life," cried the tempter; "break forth into life, liberty, and sanity. Your social happiness, your intellectual powers, your immortal interests, perhaps, depend on the choice of this moment.—There is the door, and the key is in my hand.—Choose—choose!"—"And how comes the key in your hand? and what is the condition of my liberation?" said Stanton.

* * * *

The explanation occupied several pages, which, to the torture of young Melmoth, were wholly illegible. It seemed, however, to have been rejected by Stanton with the utmost rage and horror, for Melmoth at last made out—"Begone, monster, demon!—begone to your native place. Even this mansion of horror trembles to contain you; its walls sweat, and its floors quiver, while you tread them."

* * * *

The conclusion of this extraordinary manuscript was in such a state, that, in fifteen moldy and crumbling pages, Melmoth could hardly make out that number of lines. No antiquarian, unfolding with trembling hand the calcined leaves of an Herculaneum manuscript, and hoping to discover some lost lines of the Aeneis in Virgil's own autograph, or at least some unutterable abomination of Petronius or Martial, happily elucidatory of the mysteries of the Spintriae, or the orgies of the Phallic worshipers, ever pored with more luckless diligence, or shook a head of more hopeless despondency over his task. He could but just make out what tended rather to excite than assuage that feverish thirst of curiosity which was consuming his inmost soul. The manuscript told no more of Melmoth, but mentioned that Stanton was finally liberated from his confinement—that his pursuit of Melmoth was incessant and indefatigable—that he himself allowed it to be a species of insanity—that while he acknowledged it to be the master passion, he also felt it the master torment of his life. He again visited the Continent, returned to England—pursued, inquired, traced, bribed, but in vain. The being whom he had met thrice, under circumstances so extraordinary, he was fated never to encounter again *in his lifetime*. At length, discovering that he had been born in Ireland, he resolved to go there—went, and found his pursuit again fruitless, and his inquiries unanswered. The family knew nothing of him, or at least what they knew or imagined, they prudently refused to disclose to a stranger, and Stanton departed unsatisfied. It is remarkable, that he too, as appeared from many half-obliterated pages of the manuscript, never disclosed to mortal the particulars of their conversation in the madhouse; and the slightest allusion to it threw him into fits of rage and gloom equally singular and alarming. He left the manuscript, however, in the hands of the family, possibly deeming, from their incuriosity, their apparent indifference to their relative, or their obvious unacquaintance with reading of any kind, manuscript or books, his deposit would be safe. He seems, in fact, to have acted like men, who, in distress at sea, intrust their letters and dispatches to a bottle sealed, and commit it to the waves. The last lines of the manuscript that were legible, were sufficiently extraordinary....

* * * *

"I have sought him everywhere.—The desire of meeting him once more is become as a burning fire within me—it is the necessary condition of my existence. I have vainly sought him at last in Ireland, of which I find he is a native.—Perhaps our final meeting will be in....

* * * *

Such was the conclusion of the manuscript which Melmoth found in his uncle's closet. When he had finished it, he sunk down on the table near which he had been reading it, his face hid in his folded arms, his senses reeling, his mind in a mingled state of stupor and excitement. After a few moments, he raised himself with an involuntary start, and saw the picture gazing at him from its canvas. He was within ten inches of it as he sat, and the proximity appeared increased by the strong light that was

accidentally thrown on it, and its being the only repre-
sentation of a human figure in the room. Melmoth felt for
a moment as if he were about to receive an explanation
from its lips.

He gazed on it in return—all was silent in the house—
they were alone together. The illusion subsided at length:
and as the mind rapidly passes to opposite extremes, he
remembered the injunction of his uncle to destroy the
portrait. He seized it—his hand shook at first, but the
moldering canvas appeared to assist him in the effort. He
tore it from the frame with a cry half terrific, half trium-
phant—it fell at his feet, and he shuddered as it fell.

He expected to hear some fearful sounds, some un-
imaginable breathings of prophetic horror, follow this act
of sacrilege, for such he felt it, to tear the portrait of his
ancestor from his native walls. He paused and listened:—
"There was no voice, nor any that answered;"—but as the
wrinkled and torn canvas fell to the floor, its undulations
gave the portrait the appearance of smiling. Melmoth felt
horror indescribable at this transient and imaginary re-
suscitation of the figure. He caught it up, rushed into the
next room, tore, cut, and hacked it in every direction, and
eagerly watched the fragments that burned like tinder in
the turf fire which had been lit in his room.

As Melmoth saw the last blaze, he threw himself
into bed, in hope of a deep and intense sleep. He had
done what was required of him, and felt exhausted both
in mind and body; but his slumber was not so sound as
he had hoped for. The sullen light of the turf fire, burning but never blazing, disturbed him every moment. He
turned and turned, but still there was the same red light
glaring on, but not illuminating, the dusky furniture of
the apartment. The wind was high that night, and as the

creaking door swung on its hinges, every noise seemed like the sound of a hand struggling with the lock, or of a foot pausing on the threshold. But (for Melmoth never could decide) was it in a dream or not, that he saw the figure of his ancestor appear at the door?—hesitatingly as he saw him at first on the night of his uncle's death—saw him enter the room, approach his bed, and heard him whisper, "You have burned me, then; but those are flames I can survive.—I am alive—I am beside you." Melmoth started, sprung from his bed—it was broad daylight. He looked round—there was no human being in the room but himself. He felt a slight pain in the wrist of his right arm. He looked at it, it was black and blue, as from the recent gripe of a strong hand.

MELMOTH RECONCILED

HONORÉ DE BALZAC

To Monsieur le Général Baron de Pommereul, a token
of the friendship between our fathers, which survives in
their sons.

—De Balzac.

There is a special variety of human nature obtained
in the Social Kingdom by a process analogous to that of
the gardener's craft in the Vegetable Kingdom, to wit,
by the forcing-house—a species of hybrid which can be
raised neither from seed nor from slips. This product is
known as the Cashier, an anthropomorphous growth,
watered by religious doctrine, trained up in fear of the
guillotine, pruned by vice, to flourish on a third floor with
an estimable wife by his side and an uninteresting family.
The number of cashiers in Paris must always be a prob-
lem for the physiologist. Has anyone as yet been able to
state correctly the terms of the proportion sum wherein
the cashier figures as the unknown x? Where will you
find the man who shall live with wealth, like a cat with
a caged mouse? This man, for further qualification, shall
be capable of sitting boxed in behind an iron grating
for seven or eight hours a day during seven-eighths of
the year, perched upon a cane-seated chair in a space as
narrow as a lieutenant's cabin on board a man-of-war.

Such a man must be able to defy anchylosis of the knee and thigh joints; he must have a soul above meanness, in order to live meanly; must lose all relish for money by dint of handling it. Demand this peculiar specimen of any creed, educational system, school, or institution you please, and select Paris, that city of fiery ordeals and branch establishment of hell, as the soil in which to plant the said cashier. So be it. Creeds, schools, institutions, and moral systems, all human rules and regulations, great and small, will, one after another, present much the same face that an intimate friend turns upon you when you ask him to lend you a thousand francs. With a dolorous dropping of the jaw, they indicate the guillotine, much as your friend aforesaid will furnish you with the address of the money lender, pointing you to one of the hundred gates by which a man comes to the last refuge of the destitute.

Yet Nature has her freaks in the making of a man's mind; she indulges herself and makes a few honest folk now and again, and now and then a cashier.

Wherefore, that race of corsairs whom we dignify with the title of bankers, the gentry who take out a license for which they pay a thousand crowns, as the privateer takes out his letters of marque, hold these rare products of the incubations of virtue in such esteem that they confine them in cages in their counting-houses, much as governments procure and maintain specimens of strange beasts at their own charges.

If the cashier is possessed of an imagination or of a fervid temperament; if, as will sometimes happen to the most complete cashier, he loves his wife, and that wife grows tired of her lot, has ambitions, or merely some vanity in her composition, the cashier is undone. Search the chronicles of the counting-house. You will not find a single instance of a cashier attaining *a position*, as it is called. They are sent to the hulks; they go to foreign parts; they vegetate on a second floor in the Rue Saint-Louis among the market gardens of the Marais. Some day, when the cashiers of Paris come to a sense of their real value, a cashier will be hardly obtainable for money. Still, certain it is that there are people who are fit for nothing but to be cashiers, just as the bent of a certain order of mind inevitably makes for rascality. But, oh marvel of our civilization! Society rewards virtue with an income of a hundred louis in old age, a dwelling on a second floor, bread sufficient, occasional new bandana handkerchiefs, an elderly wife and her offspring.

So much for virtue. But for the opposite course, a little boldness, a faculty for keeping on the windward side of the law, as Turenne outflanked Montecuculli, and Society will sanction the theft of millions, shower ribbons upon the thief, cram him with honors, and smother him with consideration.

Government, moreover, works harmoniously with this profoundly illogical reasoner—Society. Government levies a conscription on the young intelligence of the kingdom at the age of seventeen or eighteen, a conscription of precocious power. Great ability is prematurely exhausted by excessive brain work before it is sent up to be submitted to a process of selection. Nurserymen sort and select seeds in much the same way. To this process the Government brings professional appraisers of talent, men who can assay brains as experts assay gold at the Mint. Five hundred such heads, set afire with hope, are sent up annually by the most progressive portion of the population; and of these the Government takes one third, puts them in sacks called the Écoles, and shakes them up together for three years. Though every one of these young plants represents vast productive power, they are made, as one may say, into cashiers. They receive appointments; the rank and file of engineers is made up of them; they are employed as captains of artillery; there is no (subaltern) grade to which they may not aspire. Finally, when these men, the pick of the youth of the nation, fattened on mathematics and stuffed with knowledge, have attained the age of fifty years, they have their reward, and receive as the price of their services the third-floor lodging, the wife and family, and all the comforts that sweeten life for mediocrity. If from among this race of dupes there should escape some five or six men of genius who climb the highest heights, is it not miraculous?

This is an exact statement of the relations between Talent and Probity on the one hand, and Government and Society on the other, in an age that considers itself to be progressive. Without this prefatory explanation a recent occurrence in Paris would seem improbable; but preceded by this summing up of the situation, it will perhaps receive some thoughtful attention from minds capable of recognizing the real plague spots of our civilization, a civilization which since 1815 has been moved by the spirit of gain rather than by principles of honor.

* * * *

About five o'clock, on a dull autumn afternoon, the cashier of one of the largest banks in Paris was still at his desk, working by the light of a lamp that had been lit for some time. In accordance with the use and wont of commerce, the counting-house was in the darkest corner of the low-ceiled and far from spacious mezzanine floor, and at the very end of a passage lighted only by borrowed lights. The office doors along this corridor, each with its label, gave the place the look of a bath-house. At four o'clock the stolid porter had proclaimed, according to his orders, "The bank is closed." And by this time the departments were deserted, the letters dispatched, the clerks had taken their leave. The wives of the partners in the firm were expecting their lovers; the two bankers dining with their mistresses. Everything was in order.

The place where the strong boxes had been bedded in sheet iron was just behind the little sanctum, where the cashier was busy. Doubtless he was balancing his books. The open front gave a glimpse of a safe of hammered iron, so enormously heavy (thanks to the science of the modern inventor) that burglars could not carry it away. The door only opened at the pleasure of those who knew its password. The letter-lock was a warden who kept its own secret and could not be bribed; the mysterious word was an ingenious realization of the "Open sesame!" in the *Arabian Nights*. But even this was as nothing. A man might discover the password; but unless he knew the lock's final secret, the *ultima ratio* of this gold-guarding dragon of mechanical science, it discharged a blunderbuss at his head.

The door of the room, the walls of the room, the shutters of the windows in the room, the whole place, in fact, was lined with sheet iron a third of an inch in thickness, concealed behind the thin wooden paneling. The shutters had been closed, the door had been shut. If ever man could feel confident that he was absolutely alone, and that there was no remote possibility of being watched by prying eyes, that man was the cashier of the house of Nucingen and Company in the Rue Saint-Lazare.

Accordingly the deepest silence prevailed in that iron cave. The fire had died out in the stove, but the room was full of that tepid warmth which produces the dull heavy-headedness and nauseous queasiness of a morning after an orgy. The stove is a mesmerist that plays no small part in the reduction of bank clerks and porters to a state of idiocy.

A room with a stove in it is a retort in which the power of strong men is evaporated, where their vitality is exhausted, and their wills enfeebled. Government offices are part of a great scheme for the manufacture of the mediocrity necessary for the maintenance of a Feudal System on a pecuniary basis—and money is the foundation of the Social Contract. (See *Les Employés*.) The mephitic vapors in the atmosphere of a crowded room contribute in no small degree to bring about a gradual deterioration of intelligences, the brain that gives off the largest quantity of nitrogen asphyxiates the others, in the long run.

The cashier was a man of five and forty or thereabouts. As he sat at the table, the light from a moderator lamp shining full on his bald head and glistening fringe of iron-gray hair that surrounded it—this baldness and the round outlines of his face made his head look very like a ball. His complexion was brick-red, a few wrinkles had gathered about his eyes, but he had the smooth, plump hands of a stout man. His blue cloth coat, a little rubbed and worn, and the creases and shininess of his trousers, traces of hard wear that the clothes-brush fails to remove, would impress a superficial observer with the idea that here was a thrifty and upright human being, sufficient of the philosopher or of the aristocrat to wear shabby clothes. But, unluckily, it is easy to find penny-wise people who will prove weak, wasteful, or incompetent in the capital things of life.

The cashier wore the ribbon of the Legion of Honor at his buttonhole, for he had been a major of dragoons in the time of the Emperor. M. de Nucingen, who had been a contractor before he became a banker, had had reason in those days to know the honorable disposition of his cashier, who then occupied a high position. Reverses of fortune had befallen the major, and the banker out of regard for him paid him five hundred francs a month. The soldier had become a cashier in the year 1813, after his recovery from a wound received at Studzianka during the Retreat from Moscow, followed by six months of enforced idleness at Strasbourg, whither several officers had been transported by order of the Emperor, that they might receive skilled attention. This particular officer, Castanier by name, retired with the honorary grade of colonel, and a pension of two thousand four hundred francs.

In ten years' time the cashier had completely effaced the soldier, and Castanier inspired the banker with such trust in him, that he was associated in the transactions that went on in the private office behind his little counting-house. The baron himself had access to it by means of a secret staircase. There, matters of business were decided. It was the bolting room where proposals were sifted; the privy council chamber where the reports of the money market were analyzed; circular notes issued thence; and finally, the private ledger and the journal which summarized the work of all the departments were kept there.

Castanier had gone himself to shut the door which opened on to a staircase that led to the parlor occupied by the two bankers on the first floor of their hotel. This done, he had sat down at his desk again, and for a moment he gazed at a little collection of letters of credit drawn on the firm of Watschildine of London. Then he had taken up the pen and imitated the banker's signature upon each. *Nucingen* he wrote, and eyed the forged signatures critically to see which seemed the most perfect copy.

Suddenly he looked up as if a needle had pricked him. "You are not alone!" a boding voice seemed to cry in his heart; and indeed the forger saw a man standing at the little grated window of the counting-house, a man whose breathing was so noiseless that he did not seem to breathe at all. Castanier looked, and saw that the door at the end of the passage was wide open; the stranger must have entered by that way.

For the first time in his life the old soldier felt a sensation of dread that made him stare open-mouthed and wide-eyed at the man before him; and for that matter, the appearance of the apparition was sufficiently alarming even if unaccompanied by the mysterious circumstances of so sudden an entry. The rounded forehead, the harsh coloring of the long oval face, indicated quite as plainly as the cut of his clothes that the man was an Englishman, reeking of his native isles. You had only to look at the collar of his overcoat, at the voluminous cravat which smothered the crushed frills of a shirt front so white that it brought out the changeless leaden hue of an impassive face, and the thin red line of the lips that seemed made to suck the blood of corpses; and you could guess at once at the black gaiters buttoned up to the knee, and the half-puritanical costume of a wealthy Englishman dressed for a walking excursion. The intolerable glitter of the stranger's eyes produced a vivid and unpleasant impression, which was only deepened by the rigid outlines of his features. The dried-up, emaciated creature seemed to carry within him some gnawing thought that consumed him and could not be appeased.

He must have digested his food so rapidly that he could doubtless eat continually without bringing any trace of color into his face or features. A tun of Tokay *vin de succession* would not have caused any faltering in that piercing glance that read men's inmost thoughts, nor dethroned the merciless reasoning faculty that always seemed to go to the bottom of things. There was something of the fell and tranquil majesty of a tiger about him.

"I have come to cash this bill of exchange, sir," he said. Castanier felt the tones of his voice thrill through every nerve with a violent shock similar to that given by a discharge of electricity.

"The safe is closed," said Castanier.

"It is open," said the Englishman, looking round the counting-house. "To-morrow is Sunday, and I cannot wait. The amount is for five hundred thousand francs. You have the money there, and I must have it."

"But how did you come in, sir?"

The Englishman smiled. That smile frightened Castanier. No words could have replied more fully nor more peremptorily than that scornful and imperial curl of the stranger's lips. Castanier turned away, took up fifty packets, each containing ten thousand francs in bank notes, and held them out to the stranger, receiving in exchange for them a bill accepted by the Baron de Nucingen. A sort of convulsive tremor ran through him as he saw a red gleam in the stranger's eyes when they fell on the forged signature on the letter of credit.

"It … it wants your signature …" stammered Castanier, handing back the bill.

"Hand me your pen," answered the Englishman.

Castanier handed him the pen with which he had just committed forgery. The stranger wrote *John Melmoth*, then he returned the slip of paper and the pen to the cashier. Castanier looked at the handwriting, noticing that it sloped from right to left in the Eastern fashion, and Melmoth disappeared so noiselessly that when Castanier looked up again an exclamation broke from him, partly because the man was no longer there, partly because he felt a strange painful sensation such as our imagination might take for an effect of poison.

The pen that Melmoth had handled sent the same sickening heat through him that an emetic produces. But it seemed impossible to Castanier that the Englishman should have guessed his crime. His inward qualms he attributed to the palpitation of the heart that, according to received ideas, was sure to follow at once on such a "turn" as the stranger had given him.

"The devil take it; I am very stupid. Providence is watching over me; for if that brute had come round to see my gentlemen to-morrow, my goose would have been cooked!" said Castanier, and he burned the unsuccessful attempts at forgery in the stove.

He put the bill that he meant to take with him in an envelope, and helped himself to five hundred thousand francs in French and English bank notes from the safe, which he locked. Then he put everything in order, lit a candle, blew out the lamp, took up his hat and umbrella, and went out sedately, as usual, to leave one of the two keys of the strong room with Madame de Nucingen, in the absence of her husband the baron.

"You are in luck, M. Castanier," said the banker's wife as he entered her room; "we have a holiday on Monday; you can go into the country, or to Soizy."

"Madame, will you be so good as to tell your husband that the bill of exchange on Watschildine, which was behind time, has just been presented? The five hundred thousand francs have been paid; so I shall not come back till noon on Tuesday."

"Good-by, monsieur; I hope you will have a pleasant time."

"The same to you, madame," replied the old dragoon as he went out. He glanced as he spoke at a young man well known in fashionable society at that time, a M. de Rastignac, who was regarded as Madame de Nucingen's lover.

"Madame," remarked this latter, "the old boy looks to me as if he meant to play you some ill turn."

"Pshaw! impossible; he is too stupid."

"Piquoizeau," said the cashier, walking into the porter's room, "what made you let anybody come up after four o'clock?"

"I have been smoking a pipe here in the doorway ever since four o'clock," said the man, "and nobody has gone into the bank. Nobody has come out either except the gentlemen—"

"Are you quite sure?"

"Yes, upon my word and honor. Stay, though, at four o'clock M. Werbrust's friend came, a young fellow from Messrs. du Tillet & Co., in the Rue Joubert."

"All right," said Castanier, and he hurried away.

The sickening sensation of heat that he had felt when he took back the pen returned in greater intensity. "*Mille diables!*" thought he, as he threaded his way along the

Boulevard de Gand, "haven't I taken proper precautions? Let me think! Two clear days, Sunday and Monday, then a day of uncertainty before they begin to look for me; altogether, three days and four nights' respite. I have a couple of passports and two different disguises; is not that enough to throw the cleverest detective off the scent? On Tuesday morning I shall draw a million francs in London before the slightest suspicion has been aroused. My debts I am leaving behind for the benefit of my creditors, who will put a 'P'[1] on the bills, and I shall live comfortably in Italy for the rest of my days as the Conte Ferraro. I was alone with him when he died, poor fellow, in the marsh of Zembin, and I shall slip into his skin.... *Mille diables!* the woman who is to follow after me might give them a clew! Think of an old campaigner like me infatuated enough to tie myself to a petticoat tail!... Why take her? I must leave her behind. Yes, I could make up my mind to it; but—I know myself—I should be ass enough to go back for her. Still, nobody knows Aquilina. Shall I take her or leave her?"

"You will not take her!" cried a voice that filled Castanier with sickening dread. He turned sharply, and saw the Englishman.

"The devil is in it!" cried the cashier aloud.

Melmoth had passed his victim by this time; and if Castanier's first impulse had been to fasten a quarrel on a man who read his own thoughts, he was so much torn by opposing feelings that the immediate result was a temporary paralysis. When he resumed his walk he fell once more into that fever of irresolution which besets those who are so carried away by passion that they are ready to commit a crime, but have not sufficient strength of

---

1   Protested

character to keep it to themselves without suffering terribly in the process. So, although Castanier had made up his mind to reap the fruits of a crime which was already half executed, he hesitated to carry out his designs. For him, as for many men of mixed character in whom weakness and strength are equally blended, the least trifling consideration determines whether they shall continue to lead blameless lives or become actively criminal. In the vast masses of men enrolled in Napoleon's armies there were many who, like Castanier, possessed the purely physical courage demanded on the battlefield, yet lacked the moral courage which makes a man as great in crime as he could have been in virtue.

The letter of credit was drafted in such terms that immediately on his arrival he might draw twenty-five thousand pounds on the firm of Watschildine, the London correspondents of the house of Nucingen. The London house had been already advised of the draft about to be made upon them; he had written to them himself. He had instructed an agent (chosen at random) to take his passage in a vessel which was to leave Portsmouth with a wealthy English family on board, who were going to Italy, and the passage money had been paid in the name of the Conte Ferraro. The smallest details of the scheme had been thought out. He had arranged matters so as to divert the search that would be made for him into Belgium and Switzerland, while he himself was at sea in the English vessel. Then, by the time that Nucingen might flatter himself that he was on the track of his late cashier, the said cashier, as the Conte Ferraro, hoped to be safe in Naples. He had determined to disfigure his face in order to disguise himself the more completely, and by means of an acid to imitate the scars of smallpox. Yet, in spite of all these precautions, which surely seemed as if they must secure him complete immunity, his conscience tormented him; he was afraid. The even and peaceful life that he had led for so long had modified the morality of the camp. His life was stainless as yet; he could not sully it without a pang. So for the last time he abandoned himself to all the influences of the better self that strenuously resisted.

"Pshaw!" he said at last, at the corner of the Boulevard and the Rue Montmartre, "I will take a cab after the play this evening and go out to Versailles. A post-chaise will be ready for me at my old quartermaster's place. He would keep my secret even if a dozen men were standing ready to shoot him down. The chances are all in my favor, so far as I see; so I shall take my little Naqui with me, and I will go."

"You will not go!" exclaimed the Englishman, and the strange tones of his voice drove all the cashier's blood back to his heart.

Melmoth stepped into a tilbury which was waiting for him, and was whirled away so quickly, that when Castanier looked up he saw his foe some hundred paces away from him, and before it even crossed his mind to cut off the man's retreat the tilbury was far on its way up the Boulevard Montmartre.

"Well, upon my word, there is something supernatural about this!" said he to himself. "If I were fool enough to believe in God, I should think that He had set Saint Michael on my tracks. Suppose that the devil and the police should let me go on as I please, so as to nab me in the nick of time? Did anyone ever see the like! But there, this is folly...."

Castanier went along the Rue du Faubourg-Montmartre, slackening his pace as he neared the Rue Richer.

There, on the second floor of a block of buildings which looked out upon some gardens, lived the unconscious cause of Castanier's crime—a young woman known in the quarter as Mme. de la Garde. A concise history of certain events in the cashier's past life must be given in order to explain these facts, and to give a complete presentment of the crisis when he yielded to temptation.

Mme. de la Garde said that she was a Piedmontese. No one, not even Castanier, knew her real name. She was one of those young girls who are driven by dire misery, by inability to earn a living, or by fear of starvation, to have recourse to a trade which most of them loathe, many regard with indifference, and some few follow in obedience to the laws of their constitution. But on the brink of the gulf of prostitution in Paris, the young girl of sixteen, beautiful and pure as the Madonna, had met with Castanier. The old dragoon was too rough and homely to make his way in society, and he was tired of tramping the boulevard at night and of the kind of conquests made there by gold. For some time past he had desired to bring a certain regularity into an irregular life. He was struck by the beauty of the poor child who had drifted by chance into his arms, and his determination to rescue her from the life of the streets was half benevolent, half selfish, as some of the thoughts of the best of men are apt to be. Social conditions mingle elements of evil with the promptings of natural goodness of heart, and the mixture of motives underlying a man's intentions should be leniently judged. Castanier had just cleverness enough to be very shrewd where his own interests were concerned. So he concluded to be a philanthropist on either count, and at first made her his mistress.

"Hey! hey!" he said to himself, in his soldierly fashion, "I am an old wolf, and a sheep shall not make a fool of me. Castanier, old man, before you set up housekeeping, reconnoiter the girl's character for a bit, and see if she is a steady sort."

This irregular union gave the Piedmontese a status the most nearly approaching respectability among those which the world declines to recognize. During the first year she took the *nom de guerre* of Aquilina, one of the characters in *Venice Preserved* which she had chanced to read. She fancied that she resembled the courtesan in face and general appearance, and in a certain precocity of heart and brain of which she was conscious. When Castanier found that her life was as well regulated and virtuous as was possible for a social outlaw, he manifested a desire that they should live as husband and wife. So she took the name of Mme. de la Garde, in order to approach, as closely as Parisian usages permit, the conditions of a real marriage. As a matter of fact, many of these unfortunate girls have one fixed idea, to be looked upon as respectable middle-class women, who lead humdrum lives of faithfulness to their husbands; women who would make excellent mothers, keepers of household accounts, and menders of household linen. This longing springs from a sentiment so laudable that society should take it into consideration. But society, incorrigible as ever, will assuredly persist in regarding the married woman as a corvette duly authorized by her flag and papers to go on her own course, while the woman who is a wife in all but name is a pirate and an outlaw for lack of a document. A day came when Mme. de la Garde would fain have signed herself "Mme. Castanier." The cashier was put out by this.

"So you do not love me well enough to marry me?" she said.

Castanier did not answer; he was absorbed by his thoughts. The poor girl resigned herself to her fate. The ex-dragoon was in despair. Naqui's heart softened toward him at the sight of his trouble; she tried to soothe him, but what could she do when she did not know what ailed him? When Naqui made up her mind to know the secret, although she never asked him a question, the cashier dolefully confessed to the existence of a Mme. Castanier. This lawful wife, a thousand times accursed, was living in a humble way in Strasbourg on a small property there; he wrote to her twice a year, and kept the secret of her existence so well, that no one suspected that he was married. The reason of this reticence? If it is familiar to many military men who may chance to be in a like predicament, it is perhaps worth while to give the story.

Your genuine trooper (if it is allowable here to employ the word which in the army signifies a man who is destined to die as a captain) is a sort of serf, a part and parcel of his regiment, an essentially simple creature, and Castanier was marked out by nature as a victim to the wiles of mothers with grown-up daughters left too long on their hands. It was at Nancy, during one of those brief intervals of repose when the Imperial armies were not on active service abroad, that Castanier was so unlucky as to pay some attention to a young lady with whom he danced at a *ridotto*, the provincial name for the entertainments often given by the military to the townsfolk, or *vice versâ*, in garrison towns. A scheme for inveigling the gallant captain into matrimony was immediately set on foot, one of those schemes by which mothers secure accomplices in a human heart by touching all its motive springs, while they convert all their friends into fellow-conspirators. Like all people possessed by one idea, these ladies press everything into the service of their great project, slowly elaborating their toils, much as the ant-lion excavates its funnel in the sand and lies in wait at the bottom for its victim. Suppose that no one strays, after all, into that carefully constructed labyrinth? Suppose that the ant-lion dies of hunger and thirst in her pit? Such things may be, but if any heedless creature once enters in, it never comes out. All the wires which could be pulled to induce action on the captain's part were tried; appeals were made to the secret interested motives that always come into play in such cases; they worked on Castanier's hopes and on the weaknesses and vanity of human nature. Unluckily, he had praised the daughter to her mother when he brought her back after a waltz, a little chat followed, and then an invitation in the most natural way in the world. Once introduced into the house, the dragoon was dazzled by the hospitality of a family who appeared to conceal their real wealth beneath a show of careful economy. He was skillfully flattered on all sides, and everyone extolled for his benefit the various treasures there displayed. A neatly timed dinner, served on plate lent by an uncle, the attention shown to him by the only daughter of the house, the gossip of the town, a well-to-do sub-lieutenant who seemed likely to cut the ground from under his feet—all the innumerable snares, in short, of the provincial ant-lion were set for him, and to such good purpose, that Castanier said five years later, "To this day I do not know how it came about!"

The dragoon received fifteen thousand francs with the lady, who, after two years of marriage, became the ugliest and consequently the most peevish woman on earth. Luckily they had no children. The fair complexion (maintained by a Spartan regimen), the fresh, bright color in her face, which spoke of an engaging modesty, became overspread with blotches and pimples; her figure, which had seemed so straight, grew crooked, the angel became a suspicious and shrewish creature who drove Castanier frantic. Then the fortune took to itself wings. At length the dragoon, no longer recognizing the woman whom he had wedded, left her to live on a little property at Strasbourg, until the time when it should please God to remove her to adorn Paradise. She was one of those virtuous women who, for want of other occupation, would weary the life out of an angel with complainings, who pray till (if their prayers are heard in heaven) they must exhaust the patience of the Almighty, and say everything that is bad of their husbands in dove-like murmurs over a game of boston with their neighbors. When Aquilina learned all these troubles she clung still more affectionately to Castanier, and made him so happy, varying with woman's ingenuity the pleasures with which she filled his life, that all unwittingly she was the cause of the cashier's downfall.

Like many women who seem by nature destined to sound all the depths of love, Mme. de la Garde was disinterested. She asked neither for gold nor for jewelry, gave no thought to the future, lived entirely for the present and for the pleasures of the present. She accepted expensive ornaments and dresses, the carriage so eagerly coveted by women of her class, as one harmony the more in the picture of life. There was absolutely no vanity in her desire not to appear at a better advantage but to look the fairer, and, moreover, no woman could live without luxuries more cheerfully. When a man of generous nature (and military men are mostly of this stamp) meets with such a woman, he feels a sort of exasperation at finding himself her debtor in generosity. He feels that he could stop a mail coach to obtain money for her if he has not sufficient for her whims. He will commit a crime if so he may be great and noble in the eyes of some woman or of his special public; such is the nature of the man. Such a lover is like a gambler who would be dishonored in his own eyes if he did not repay the sum he borrowed from a waiter in a gaming house; but will shrink from no crime, will leave his wife and children without a penny, and rob and murder, if so he may come to the gaming table with a full purse, and his honor remain untarnished among the frequenters of that fatal abode. So it was with Castanier.

He had begun by installing Aquilina in a modest fourth-floor dwelling, the furniture being of the simplest kind. But when he saw the girl's beauty and great qualities, when he had known inexpressible and unlooked-for happiness with her, he began to dote upon her, and longed to adorn his idol. Then Aquilina's toilet was so comically out of keeping with her poor abode, that for both their sakes it was clearly incumbent on him to move. The change swallowed up almost all Castanier's savings, for he furnished his domestic paradise with all the prodigality that is lavished on a kept mistress. A pretty woman must have everything pretty about her; the unity of charm in the woman and her surroundings singles her out from among her sex. This sentiment of homogeneity indeed, though it has frequently escaped the attention of observers, is instinctive in human nature; and the same prompting leads elderly spinsters to surround themselves with dreary relies of the past. But the lovely Piedmontese must have the newest and latest fashions, and all that was daintiest and prettiest in stuffs for hangings, in silks or jewelry, in fine china and other brittle and fragile wares. She asked for nothing; but when she was called upon to make a choice, when Castanier asked her, "Which do you like?" she would answer, "Why, this is the nicest!" Love never counts the cost, and Castanier therefore always took the "nicest."

When once the standard had been set up, there was nothing for it but everything in the household must be in conformity, from the linen, plate, and crystal through a thousand and one items of expenditure down to the pots and pans in the kitchen. Castanier had meant to "do things simply," as the saying goes, but he gradually found himself more and more in debt. One expense entailed another. The clock called for candle sconces. Fires must be lighted in the ornamental grates, but the curtains and hangings were too fresh and delicate to be soiled by smuts, so they must be replaced by patent and elaborate fireplaces, warranted to give out no smoke, recent inventions of the people who are clever at drawing up a prospectus. Then Aquilina found it so nice to run about barefooted on the carpet in her room that Castanier must have soft carpets laid everywhere for the pleasure of playing with Naqui. A bathroom, too, was built for her, everything to the end that she might be more comfortable.

Shopkeepers, workmen, and manufacturers in Paris have a mysterious knack of enlarging a hole in a man's purse. They cannot give the price of anything upon inquiry; and as the paroxysm of longing cannot abide delay, orders are given by the feeble light of an approximate estimate of cost. The same people never send in the bills at once, but ply the purchaser with furniture till his head spins. Everything is so pretty, so charming; and everyone is satisfied.

A few months later the obliging furniture dealers are metamorphosed, and reappear in the shape of alarming totals on invoices that fill the soul with their horrid clamor; they are in urgent want of the money; they are, as you may say, on the brink of bankruptcy, their tears flow, it is heartrending to hear them! And then—the gulf yawns and gives up serried columns of figures marching four deep; when as a matter of fact they should have issued innocently three by three.

Before Castanier had any idea of how much he had spent, he had arranged for Aquilina to have a carriage from a livery stable when she went out, instead of a cab. Castanier was a gourmand; he engaged an excellent cook; and Aquilina, to please him, had herself made the purchases of early fruit and vegetables, rare delicacies, and exquisite wines. But, as Aquilina had nothing of her own, these gifts of hers, so precious by reason of the thought and tact and graciousness that prompted them, were no less a drain upon Castanier's purse; he did not like his Naqui to be without money, and Naqui could not keep money in her pocket. So the table was a heavy item of expenditure for a man with Castanier's income. The ex-dragoon was compelled to resort to various shifts for obtaining money, for he could not bring himself to renounce this delightful life. He loved the woman too well to cross the freaks of the mistress. He was one of those men who, through self-love or through weakness of character, can refuse nothing to a woman; false shame overpowers them, and they rather face ruin than make the admissions: "I cannot—" "My means will not permit—" "I cannot afford—"

When, therefore, Castanier saw that if he meant to emerge from the abyss of debt into which he had plunged, he must part with Aquilina and live upon bread and water, he was so unable to do without her or to change his habits of life, that daily he put off his plans of reform until the morrow. The debts were pressing, and he began by borrowing money. His position and previous character inspired confidence, and of this he took advantage to devise a system of borrowing money as he required it. Then, as the total amount of debt rapidly increased, he had recourse to those commercial inventions known as *accommodation bills*. This form of bill does not represent goods or other value received, and the first indorser pays the amount named for the obliging person who accepts it. This species of fraud is tolerated because it is impossible to detect it, and, moreover, it is an imaginary fraud which only becomes real if payment is ultimately refused.

When at length it was evidently impossible to borrow any longer, whether because the amount of the debt was now so greatly increased, or because Castanier was unable to pay the large amount of interest on the aforesaid sums of money, the cashier saw bankruptcy before him. On making this discovery, he decided for a fraudulent bankruptcy rather than an ordinary failure, and preferred a crime to a misdemeanor. He determined, after the fashion of the celebrated cashier of the Royal Treasury, to abuse the trust deservedly won, and to increase the number of his creditors by making a final loan of the sum sufficient to keep him in comfort in a foreign country for the rest of his days. All this, as has been seen, he had prepared to do.

Aquilina knew nothing of the irksome cares of this life; she enjoyed her existence, as many a woman does, making no inquiry as to where the money came from, even as sundry other folk will eat their buttered rolls untroubled by any restless spirit of curiosity as to the culture and growth of wheat; but as the labor and miscalculations of agriculture lie on the other side of the baker's oven, so, beneath the unappreciated luxury of many a Parisian household lie intolerable anxieties and exorbitant toil.

While Castanier was enduring the torture of the strain, and his thoughts were full of the deed that should change his whole life, Aquilina was lying luxuriously back in a great armchair by the fireside, beguiling the time by chatting with her waiting-maid. As frequently happens in such cases, the maid had become the mistress's confidante, Jenny having first assured herself that her mistress's ascendancy over Castanier was complete.

What are we to do this evening? Léon seems determined to come," Mme. de la Garde was saying, as she read a passionate epistle indicted upon a faint gray note paper.

"Here is the master!" said Jenny.

Castanier came in. Aquilina, nowise disconcerted, crumpled up the letter, took it with the tongs, and held it in the flames.

"So that is what you do with your love letters, is it?" asked Castanier.

"Oh, goodness, yes," said Aquilina; "is it not the best way of keeping them safe? Besides, fire should go to the fire, as water makes for the river."

"You are talking as if it were a real love letter, Naqui—"

"Well, am I not handsome enough to receive them?" she said, holding up her forehead for a kiss. There was a carelessness in her manner that would have told any man less blind than Castanier that it was only a piece of conjugal duty, as it were, to give this joy to the cashier; but use and wont had brought Castanier to the point where clear-sightedness is no longer possible for love.

"I have taken a box at the Gymnase this evening," he said; "let us have dinner early, and then we need not dine in a hurry."

"Go and take Jenny. I am tired of plays. I do not know what is the matter with me this evening; I would rather stay here by the fire."

"Come, all the same though, Naqui; I shall not be here to bore you much longer. Yes, Quiqui, I am going to start to-night, and it will be some time before I come back again. I am leaving everything in your charge. Will you keep your heart for me too?"

"Neither my heart nor anything else," she said; "but when you come back again, Naqui will still be Naqui for you."

"Well, this is frankness. So you would not follow me?"

"No."

"Why not?"

"Eh! why, how can I leave the lover who writes me such sweet little notes?" she asked, pointing to the blackened scrap of paper with a mocking smile.

"Is there any truth in it?" asked Castanier. "Have you really a lover?"

"Really!" cried Aquilina; "and have you never given it a serious thought, dear? To begin with, you are fifty years old. Then you have just the sort of face to put on a fruit stall; if the woman tried to sell you for a pumpkin, no one would contradict her. You puff and blow like a seal when you come upstairs; your paunch rises and falls like the diamond on a woman's forehead! It is pretty plain that you served in the dragoons; you are a very ugly-looking old man. Fiddle-de-dee. If you have any mind to keep my respect, I recommend you not to add imbecility to these qualities by imagining that such a girl as I am will be content with your asthmatic love, and not look for youth and good looks and pleasure by way of variety—"

"Aquilina! you are laughing, of course?"

"Oh, very well; and are you not laughing too? Do you take me for a fool, telling me that you are going away? 'I am going to start to-night!'" she said, mimicking his tones. "Stuff and nonsense! Would you talk like that if you were really going away from your Naqui? You would cry, like the booby that you are!"

"After all, if I go, will you follow?" he asked.

"Tell me first whether this journey of yours is a bad joke or not."

"Yes, seriously, I am going."

"Well, then, seriously, I shall stay. A pleasant journey to you, my boy! I will wait till you come back. I would sooner take leave of life than take leave of my dear, cozy Paris—"

"Will you not come to Italy, to Naples, and lead a pleasant life there—a delicious, luxurious life, with this stout old fogey of yours, who puffs and blows like a seal?"

"No."

"Ungrateful girl!"

"Ungrateful?" she cried, rising to her feet. "I might leave this house this moment and take nothing out of it but myself. I shall have given you all the treasures a young girl can give, and something that not every drop in your veins and mine can ever give me back. If, by any means whatever, by selling my hopes of eternity, for instance, I could recover my past self, body as soul (for I have, perhaps, redeemed my soul), and be pure as a lily for my lover I would not hesitate a moment! What sort of devotion has rewarded mine? You have housed and fed me, just as you give a dog food and a kennel because he is a protection to the house, and he may take kicks when we are out of humor, and lick our hands as soon as we are pleased to call to him. And which of us two will have been the more generous?"

"Oh! dear child, do you not see that I am joking?" returned Castanier. "I am going on a short journey; I shall not be away for very long. But come with me to the Gymnase; I shall start just before midnight, after I have had time to say good-by to you."

"Poor pet! so you are really going, are you?" she said. She put her arms round his neck, and drew down his head against her bodice.

"You are smothering me!" cried Castanier, with his face buried in Aquilina's breast. That damsel turned to say in Jenny's ear, "Go to Léon, and tell him not to come till one o'clock. If you do not find him, and he comes here during the leave-taking, keep him in your room.—Well," she went on, setting free Castanier, and giving a tweak to the tip of his nose, "never mind, handsomest of seals that you are. I will go to the theater with you this evening. But all in good time; let us have dinner! There is a nice little dinner for you—just what you like."

"It is very hard to part from such a woman as you!" exclaimed Castanier.

"Very well then, why do you go?" asked she.

"Ah! why? why? If I were to begin to explain the reasons why, I must tell you things that would prove to you that I love you almost to madness. Ah! if you have sacrificed your honor for me, I have sold mine for you; we are quits. Is that love?"

"What is all this about?" said she. "Come, now, promise me that if I had a lover you would still love me as a father; that would be love! Come, now, promise it at once, and give us your fist upon it."

"I should kill you," and Castanier smiled as he spoke.

They sat down to the dinner table, and went thence to the Gymnase. When the first part of the performance was over, it occurred to Castanier to show himself to some of his acquaintances in the house, so as to turn away any suspicion of his departure. He left Mme. de la Garde in the corner box where she was seated, according to her modest wont, and went to walk up and down in the lobby. He had not gone many paces before he saw the Englishman, and with a sudden return of the sickening sensation of heat that once before had vibrated through him, and of the terror that he had felt already, he stood face to face with Melmoth.

"Forger!"

At the word, Castanier glanced round at the people who were moving about them. He fancied that he could see astonishment and curiosity in their eyes, and wishing to be rid of this Englishman at once, he raised his hand to strike him—and felt his arm paralyzed by some invisible power that sapped his strength and nailed him to the spot. He allowed the stranger to take him by the arm, and they walked together to the greenroom like two friends.

"Who is strong enough to resist me?" said the Englishman, addressing him. "Do you not know that everything here on earth must obey me, that it is in my power to do everything? I read men's thoughts, I see the future, and I know the past. I am here, and I can be elsewhere also. Time and space and distance are nothing to me. The whole world is at my beck and call. I have the power of continual enjoyment and of giving joy. I can see through walls, discover hidden treasures, and fill my hands with them. Palaces arise at my nod, and my architect makes no mistakes. I can make all lands break forth into blossom, heap up their gold and precious stones, and surround myself with fair women and ever new faces; everything is yielded up to my will. I could gamble on the Stock Exchange, and my speculations would be infallible; but a man who can find the hoards that misers have hidden in the earth need not trouble himself about stocks. Feel the strength of the hand that grasps you; poor wretch, doomed to shame! Try to bend the arm of iron! try to soften the adamantine heart! Fly from me if you dare! You would hear my voice in the depths of the caves that lie under the Seine; you might hide in the Catacombs, but would you not see me there? My voice could be heard through the sound of the thunder, my eyes shine as brightly as the sun, for I am the peer of Lucifer!"

Castanier heard the terrible words, and felt no protest nor contradiction within himself. He walked side by side with the Englishman, and had no power to leave him.

"You are mine; you have just committed a crime. I have found at last the mate whom I have sought. Have you a mind to learn your destiny? Aha! you came here to see a play, and you shall see a play—nay, two. Come. Present me to Mme. de la Garde as one of your best friends. Am I not your last hope of escape?"

Castanier, followed by the stranger, returned to his box; and in accordance with the order he had just received, he hastened to introduce Melmoth to Mme. de la Garde. Aquilina seemed to be not in the least surprised. The Englishman declined to take a seat in front, and Castanier was once more beside his mistress; the man's slightest wish must be obeyed. The last piece was about to begin, for, at that time, small theaters only gave three pieces. One of the actors had made the Gymnase the fashion, and that evening Perlet (the actor in question) was to play in a vaudeville called *Le Comédien d'Étampes*, in which he filled four different parts.

When the curtain rose, the stranger stretched out his hand over the crowded house. Castanier's cry of terror died away, for the walls of his throat seemed glued together as Melmoth pointed to the stage, and the cashier knew that the play had been changed at the Englishman's desire.

He saw the strong room at the bank; he saw the Baron de Nucingen in conference with a police officer from the prefecture, who was informing him of Castanier's conduct, explaining that the cashier had absconded with money taken from the safe, giving the history of the forged signature. The information was put in writing; the document signed and duly dispatched to the public prosecutor.

"Are we in time, do you think?" asked Nucingen.

"Yes," said the agent of police; "he is at the Gymnase, and has no suspicion of anything."

Castanier fidgeted on his chair, and made as if he would leave the theater, but Melmoth's hand lay on his shoulder, and he was obliged to sit and watch; the hideous power of the man produced an effect like that of nightmare, and he could not move a limb. Nay, the man himself was the nightmare; his presence weighed heavily on his victim like a poisoned atmosphere. When the wretched cashier turned to implore the Englishman's mercy, he met those blazing eyes that discharged electric currents, which pierced through him and transfixed him like darts of steel.

"What have I done to you?" he said, in his prostrate helplessness, and he breathed hard like a stag at the water's edge. "What do you want of me?"

"Look!" cried Melmoth.

Castanier looked at the stage. The scene had been changed. The play seemed to be over, and Castanier beheld himself stepping from the carriage with Aquilina; but as he entered the courtyard of the house in the Rue Richer, the scene again was suddenly changed, and he saw his own house. Jenny was chatting by the fire in her mistress's room with a subaltern officer of a line regiment then stationed at Paris.

"He is going, is he?" said the sergeant, who seemed to belong to a family in easy circumstances; "I can be happy at my ease! I love Aquilina too well to allow her to belong to that old toad! I, myself, am going to marry Mme. de la Garde!" cried the sergeant.

"Old toad!" Castanier murmured piteously.

"Here come the master and mistress; hide yourself! Stay, get in here, Monsieur Léon," said Jenny. "The master won't stay here for very long."

Castanier watched the sergeant hide himself among Aquilina's gowns in her dressing room. Almost immediately he himself appeared upon the scene, and took leave of his mistress, who made fun of him in "asides" to Jenny, while she uttered the sweetest and tenderest words in his ears. She wept with one side of her face, and laughed with the other. The audience called for an encore.

"Accursed creature!" cried Castanier from his box.

Aquilina was laughing till the tears came into her eyes.

"Goodness!" she cried, "how funny Perlet is as the Englishwoman!... Why don't you laugh? Everyone else in the house is laughing. Laugh, dear!" she said to Castanier.

Melmoth burst out laughing, and the unhappy cashier shuddered. The Englishman's laughter wrung his heart and tortured his brain; it was as if a surgeon had bored his skull with a red-hot iron.

"Laughing! are they laughing?" stammered Castanier.

He did not see the prim English lady whom Perlet was acting with such ludicrous effect, nor hear the English-French that had filled the house with roars of laughter; instead of all this, he beheld himself hurrying from the Rue Richer, hailing a cab on the Boulevard, bargaining with the man to take him to Versailles. Then once more the scene changed. He recognized the sorry inn at the corner of the Rue de l'Orangerie and the Rue des Récollets, which was kept by his old quartermaster. It was two o'clock in the morning, the most perfect stillness prevailed, no one was there to watch his movements. The post-horses were put into the carriage (it came from a house in the Avenue de Paris in which an Englishman lived, and had been ordered in the foreigner's name to avoid raising suspicion). Castanier saw that he had his bills and his passports, stepped into the carriage, and set out. But at the barrier he saw two gendarmes lying in wait for the carriage. A cry of horror burst from him, but Melmoth gave him a glance, and again the sound died in his throat.

"Keep your eyes on the stage, and be quiet!" said the Englishman.

In another moment Castanier saw himself flung into prison at the Conciergerie; and in the fifth act of the drama, entitled *The Cashier*, he saw himself, in three months' time, condemned to twenty years of penal servitude. Again a cry broke from him. He was exposed upon the Place du Palais-de-Justice, and the executioner branded him with a red-hot iron. Then came the last scene of all; among some sixty convicts in the prison yard of the Bicêtre, he was awaiting his turn to have the irons riveted on his limbs.

"Dear me! I cannot laugh any more!…" said Aquilina. "You are very solemn, dear boy; what can be the matter? The gentleman has gone."

"A word with you, Castanier," said Melmoth when the piece was at an end, and the attendant was fastening Mme. de la Garde's cloak.

The corridor was crowded, and escape impossible.

"Very well, what is it?"

"No human power can hinder you from taking Aquilina home, and going next to Versailles, there to be arrested."

"How so?"

"Because you are in a hand that will never relax its grasp," returned the Englishman.

Castanier longed for the power to utter some word that should blot him out from among living men and hide him in the lowest depths of hell.

"Suppose that the devil were to make a bid for your soul, would you not give it to him now in exchange for the power of God? One single word, and those five hundred thousand francs shall be back in the Baron de Nucingen's safe; then you can tear up your letter of credit, and all traces of your crime will be obliterated. Moreover, you would have gold in torrents. You hardly believe in anything perhaps? Well, if all this comes to pass, you will believe at least in the devil."

"If it were only possible!" said Castanier joyfully.

"The man who can do it all gives you his word that it is possible," answered the Englishman.

Melmoth, Castanier, and Mme. de la Garde were standing out in the Boulevard when Melmoth raised his arm. A drizzling rain was falling, the streets were muddy, the air was close, there was thick darkness overhead; but in a moment, as the arm was outstretched, Paris was filled with sunlight; it was high noon on a bright July day. The trees were covered with leaves; a double stream of joyous holiday makers strolled beneath them. Sellers of licorice water shouted their cool drinks. Splendid carriages rolled past along the streets. A cry of terror broke from the cashier, and at that cry rain and darkness once more settled down upon the Boulevard.

Mme. de la Garde had stepped into the carriage. "Do be quick, dear!" she cried; "either come in or stay out. Really, you are as dull as ditch-water this evening—"

"What must I do?" Castanier asked of Melmoth.

"Would you like to take my place?" inquired the Englishman.

"Yes."

"Very well, then; I will be at your house in a few moments."

"By the bye, Castanier, you are rather off your balance," Aquilina remarked. "There is some mischief brewing; you were quite melancholy and thoughtful all through the play. Do you want anything that I can give you, dear? Tell me."

"I am waiting till we are at home to know whether you love me."

"You need not wait till then," she said, throwing her arms round his neck. "There!" she said, as she embraced him, passionately to all appearance, and plied him with the coaxing caresses that are part of the business of such a life as hers, like stage action for an actress.

"Where is the music?" asked Castanier.

"What next? Only think of your hearing music now!"

"Heavenly music!" he went on. "The sounds seem to come from above."

"What? You have always refused to give me a box at the Italiens because you could not abide music, and are you turning music-mad at this time of day? Mad—that you are! The music is inside your own noddle, old addle-pate!" she went on, as she took his head in her hands and rocked it to and fro on her shoulder. "Tell me now, old man; isn't it the creaking of the wheels that sings in your ears?"

"Just listen, Naqui! If the angels make music for God Almighty, it must be such music as this that I am drinking in at every pore, rather than hearing. I do not know how to tell you about it; it is as sweet as honey water!"

"Why, of course, they have music in heaven, for the angels in all the pictures have harps in their hands. He is mad, upon my word!" she said to herself, as she saw Castanier's attitude; he looked like an opium eater in a blissful trance.

They reached the house. Castanier, absorbed by the thought of all that he had just heard and seen, knew not whether to believe it or no; he was like a drunken man, and utterly unable to think connectedly. He came to himself in Aquilina's room, whither he had been supported by the united efforts of his mistress, the porter, and Jenny; for he had fainted as he stepped from the carriage.

"*He* will be here directly! Oh, my friends, my friends!" he cried, and he flung himself despairingly into the depths of a low chair beside the fire.

Jenny heard the bell as he spoke, and admitted the Englishman. She announced that "a gentleman had come who had made an appointment with the master," when Melmoth suddenly appeared, and deep silence followed. He looked at the porter—the porter went; he looked at Jenny—and Jenny went likewise.

"Madame," said Melmoth, turning to Aquilina, "with your permission, we will conclude a piece of urgent business."

He took Castanier's hand, and Castanier rose, and the two men went into the drawing-room. There was no light in the room, but Melmoth's eyes lit up the thickest darkness. The gaze of those strange eyes had left Aquilina like one spellbound; she was helpless, unable to take any thought for her lover; moreover, she believed him to be safe in Jenny's room, whereas their early return had taken the waiting woman by surprise, and she had hidden the officer in the dressing room. It had all happened exactly as in the drama that Melmoth had displayed for his victim. Presently the house door was slammed violently, and Castanier reappeared.

"What ails you?" cried the horror-struck Aquilina.

There was a change in the cashier's appearance. A strange pallor overspread his once rubicund countenance; it wore the peculiarly sinister and stony look of the mysterious visitor. The sullen glare of his eyes was intolerable, the fierce light in them seemed to scorch. The man who had looked so good-humored and good-natured had suddenly grown tyrannical and proud. The courtesan thought that Castanier had grown thinner; there was a terrible majesty in his brow; it was as if a dragon breathed forth a malignant influence that weighed upon the others like a close, heavy atmosphere. For a moment Aquilina knew not what to do.

"What passed between you and that diabolical-looking man in those few minutes?" she asked at length.

"I have sold my soul to him. I feel it; I am no longer the same. He has taken my *self*, and given me his soul in exchange."

"What?"

"You would not understand it at all.… Ah! he was right," Castanier went on, "the fiend was right! I see everything and know all things.—You have been deceiving me!"

Aquilina turned cold with terror. Castanier lighted a candle and went into the dressing room. The unhappy girl followed him in dazed bewilderment, and great was her astonishment when Castanier drew the dresses that hung there aside and disclosed the sergeant.

"Come out, my boy," said the cashier; and, taking Léon by a button of his overcoat, he drew the officer into his room.

The Piedmontese, haggard and desperate, had flung herself into her easy chair. Castanier seated himself on a sofa by the fire, and left Aquilina's lover in a standing position.

"You have been in the army," said Léon; "I am ready to give you satisfaction."

"You are a fool," said Castanier dryly. "I have no occasion to fight. I could kill you by a look if I had any mind to do it. I will tell you what it is, youngster; why should I kill you? I can see a red line round your neck—the guillotine is waiting for you. Yes, you will end in the Place de Grève. You are the headsman's property! there is no escape for you. You belong to a *vendita* of the Carbonari. You are plotting against the Government."

"You did not tell me that," cried the Piedmontese, turning to Léon.

"So you do not know that the Minister decided this morning to put down your Society?" the cashier continued. "The Procureur-Général has a list of your names. You have been betrayed. They are busy drawing up the indictment at this moment."

"Then was it you who betrayed him?" cried Aquilina, and with a hoarse sound in her throat like the growl of a tigress she rose to her feet; she seemed as if she would tear Castanier in pieces.

"You know me too well to believe it," Castanier retorted. Aquilina was benumbed by his coolness.

"Then how did you know it?" she murmured.

"I did not know it until I went into the drawing-room; now I know it—now I see and know all things, and can do all things."

The sergeant was overcome with amazement.

"Very well then, save him, save him, dear!" cried the girl, flinging herself at Castanier's feet. "If nothing is impossible to you, save him! I will love you, I will adore you, I will be your slave and not your mistress. I will obey your wildest whims; you shall do as you will with me. Yes, yes, I will give you more than love; you shall have a daughter's devotion as well as ... Rodolphe! why will you not understand! After all, however violent my passions may be, I shall be yours forever! What should I say to persuade you? I will invent pleasures ... I ... Great heavens! one moment! whatever you shall ask of me—to fling myself from the window, for instance—you will need to say but one word, 'Léon!' and I will plunge down into hell. I would bear any torture, any pain of body or soul, anything you might inflict upon me!"

Castanier heard her with indifference. For all answer, he indicated Léon to her with a fiendish laugh.

"The guillotine is waiting for him," he repeated.

"No, no, no! He shall not leave this house. I will save him!" she cried. "Yes; I will kill anyone who lays a finger upon him! Why will you not save him?" she shrieked aloud; her eyes were blazing, her hair unbound. "Can you save him?"

"I can do everything."

"Why do you not save him?"

"Why?" shouted Castanier, and his voice made the ceiling ring.—"Eh! it is my revenge! Doing evil is my trade!"

"Die?" said Aquilina; "must he die, my lover? Is it possible?"

She sprang up and snatched a stiletto from a basket that stood on the chest of drawers and went to Castanier, who began to laugh.

"You know very well that steel cannot hurt me now—"

Aquilina's arm suddenly dropped like a snapped harp string.

"Out with you, my good friend," said the cashier, turning to the sergeant, "and go about your business."

He held out his hand; the other felt Castanier's superior power, and could not choose but obey.

"This house is mine; I could send for the commissary of police if I chose, and give you up as a man who has hidden himself on my premises, but I would rather let you go; I am a fiend, I am not a spy."

"I shall follow him!" said Aquilina.

"Then follow him," returned Castanier.—"Here, Jenny—"

Jenny appeared.

"Tell the porter to hail a cab for them.—Here, Naqui," said Castanier, drawing a bundle of banknotes from his pocket; "you shall not go away like a pauper from a man who loves you still."

He held out three hundred thousand francs. Aquilina took the notes, flung them on the floor, spat on them, and trampled upon them in a frenzy of despair.

"We will leave this house on foot," she cried, "without a farthing of your money.—Jenny, stay where you are."

"Good evening!" answered the cashier, as he gathered up the notes again. "I have come back from my journey.—Jenny," he added, looking at the bewildered waiting maid, "you seem to me to be a good sort of girl. You have no mistress now. Come here. This evening you shall have a master."

Aquilina, who felt safe nowhere, went at once with the sergeant to the house of one of her friends. But all Léon's movements were suspiciously watched by the police, and after a time he and three of his friends were arrested. The whole story may be found in the newspapers of that day.

* * * *

Castanier felt that he had undergone a mental as well as a physical transformation. The Castanier of old no longer existed—the boy, the young Lothario, the soldier who had proved his courage, who had been tricked into a marriage and disillusioned, the cashier, the passionate lover who had committed a crime for Aquilina's sake. His inmost nature had suddenly asserted itself. His brain had expanded, his senses had developed. His thoughts comprehended the whole world; he saw all the things of earth as if he had been raised to some high pinnacle above the world.

Until that evening at the play he had loved Aquilina to distraction. Rather than give her up he would have shut his eyes to her infidelities; and now all that blind passion had passed away as a cloud vanishes in the sunlight.

Jenny was delighted to succeed to her mistress's position and fortune, and did the cashier's will in all things; but Castanier, who could read the inmost thoughts of the soul, discovered the real motive underlying this purely physical devotion. He amused himself with her, however, like a mischievous child who greedily sucks the juice of the cherry and flings away the stone. The next morning at breakfast time, when she was fully convinced that she was a lady and the mistress of the house, Castanier uttered one by one the thoughts that filled her mind as she drank her coffee.

"Do you know what you are thinking, child?" he said, smiling. "I will tell you: 'So all that lovely rosewood furniture that I coveted so much, and the pretty dresses that I used to try on, are mine now! All on easy terms that madame refused, I do not know why. My word! if I might drive about in a carriage, have jewels and pretty things, a box at the theater, and put something by! with me he should lead a life of pleasure fit to kill him if he were not as strong as a Turk! I never saw such a man!'—Was not that just what you were thinking?" he went on, and something in his voice made Jenny turn pale. "Well, yes, child; you could not stand it, and I am sending you away for your own good; you would perish in the attempt. Come, let us part good friends," and he coolly dismissed her with a very small sum of money.

The first use that Castanier had promised himself that he would make of the terrible power bought at the price of his eternal happiness, was the full and complete indulgence of all his tastes.

He first put his affairs in order, readily settled his account with M. de Nucingen, who found a worthy German to succeed him, and then determined on a carouse worthy of the palmiest days of the Roman Empire. He plunged into dissipation as recklessly as Belshazzar of old went to that last feast in Babylon. Like Belshazzar, he saw clearly through his revels a gleaming hand that traced his doom in letters of flame, not on the narrow walls of the banqueting chamber, but over the vast spaces of heaven that the rainbow spans. His feast was not, indeed, an orgy confined within the limits of a banquet, for he squandered all the powers of soul and body in exhausting all the pleasures of earth. The table was in some sort earth itself, the earth that trembled beneath his feet. He was the last festival of the reckless spendthrift who has thrown all prudence to the winds. The devil had given him the key of the storehouse of human pleasures; he had filled and refilled his hands, and he was fast nearing the bottom. In a moment he had felt all that that enormous power could accomplish; in a moment he had exercised it, proved it, wearied of it. What had hitherto been the sum of human desires became as nothing. So often it happens that with possession the vast poetry of desire must end, and the thing possessed is seldom the thing that we dreamed of.

Beneath Melmoth's omnipotence lurked this tragical anticlimax of so many a passion, and now the inanity of human nature was revealed to his successor, to whom infinite power brought Nothingness as a dowry.

To come to a clear understanding of Castanier's strange position, it must be borne in mind how suddenly these revolutions of thought and feeling had been wrought; how quickly they had succeeded each other; and of these things it is hard to give any idea to those who have never broken the prison bonds of time, and space, and distance. His relation to the world without had been entirely changed with the expansion of his faculties.

Like Melmoth himself, Castanier could travel in a few moments over the fertile plains of India, could soar on the wings of demons above African desert spaces, or skim the surface of the seas. The same insight that could read the inmost thoughts of others, could apprehend at a glance the nature of any material object, just as he caught as it were all flavors at once upon his tongue. He took his pleasure like a despot; a blow of the ax felled the tree that he might eat its fruits. The transitions, the alternations that measure joy and pain, and diversify human happiness, no longer existed for him. He had so completely glutted his appetites that pleasure must overpass the limits of pleasure to tickle a palate cloyed with satiety, and suddenly grown fastidious beyond all measure, so that ordinary pleasures became distasteful. Conscious that at will he was the master of all the women that he could desire, knowing that his power was irresistible, he did not care to exercise it; they were pliant to his unexpressed wishes, to his most extravagant caprices, until he felt a horrible thirst for love, and would have love beyond their power to give.

The world refused him nothing save faith and prayer, the soothing and consoling love that is not of this world. He was obeyed—it was a horrible position.

The torrents of pain, and pleasure, and thought that shook his soul and his bodily frame would have overwhelmed the strongest human being; but in him there was a power of vitality proportioned to the power of the sensations that assailed him. He felt within him a vague immensity of longing that earth could not satisfy. He spent his days on outspread wings, longing to traverse the luminous fields of space to other spheres that he knew afar by intuitive perception, a clear and hopeless knowledge. His soul dried up within him, for he hungered and thirsted after things that can neither be drunk nor eaten, but for which he could not choose but crave. His lips, like Melmoth's, burned with desire; he panted for the unknown, for he knew all things.

The mechanism and the scheme of the world was apparent to him, and its working interested him no longer; he did not long disguise the profound scorn that makes of a man of extraordinary powers a sphinx who knows everything and says nothing, and sees all things with an unmoved countenance. He felt not the slightest wish to communicate his knowledge to other men. He was rich with all the wealth of the world, with one effort he could make the circle of the globe, and riches and power were meaningless for him. He felt the awful melancholy of omnipotence, a melancholy which Satan and God relieve by the exercise of infinite power in mysterious ways known to them alone. Castanier had not, like his Master, the inextinguishable energy of hate and malice; he felt that he was a devil, but a devil whose time was not yet come, while Satan is a devil through all eternity, and being damned beyond redemption, delights to stir up the world, like a dungheap, with his triple fork and to thwart therein the designs of God. But Castanier, for his misfortune, had one hope left.

If in a moment he could move from one pole to the other as a bird springs restlessly from side to side in its cage, when, like the bird, he had crossed his prison, he saw the vast immensity of space beyond it. That vision of the Infinite left him forever unable to see humanity and its affairs as other men saw them. The insensate fools who long for the power of the Devil gauge its desirability from a human standpoint; they do not see that with the Devil's power they will likewise assume his thoughts, and that they will be doomed to remain as men among creatures who will no longer understand them. The Nero unknown to history who dreams of setting Paris on fire for his private entertainment, like an exhibition of a burning house on the boards of a theater, does not suspect that if he had that power, Paris would become for him as little interesting as an ant heap by the roadside to a hurrying passer-by. The circle of the sciences was for Castanier something like a logogriph for a man who does not know the key to it. Kings and Governments were despicable in his eyes. His great debauch had been in some sort a deplorable farewell to his life as a man. The earth had grown too narrow for him, for the infernal gifts laid bare for him the secrets of creation—he saw the cause and foresaw its end. He was shut out from all that men call "heaven" in all languages under the sun; he could no longer think of heaven.

Then he came to understand the look on his predecessor's face and the drying up of the life within; then he knew all that was meant by the baffled hope that gleamed in Melmoth's eyes; he, too, knew the thirst that burned those red lips, and the agony of a continual struggle between two natures grown to giant size. Even yet he might be an angel, and he knew himself to be a fiend. His was the fate of a sweet and gentle creature that a wizard's malice has imprisoned in a misshapen form, entrapping it by a pact, so that another's will must set it free from its detested envelope.

As a deception only increases the ardor with which a man of really great nature explores the infinite of sentiment in a woman's heart, so Castanier awoke to find that one idea lay like a weight upon his soul, an idea which was perhaps the key to loftier spheres. The very fact that he had bartered away his eternal happiness led him to dwell in thought upon the future of those who pray and believe. On the morrow of his debauch, when he entered into the sober possession of his power, this idea made him feel himself a prisoner; he knew the burden of the woe that poets, and prophets, and great oracles of faith have set forth for us in such mighty words; he felt the point of the Flaming Sword plunged into his side, and hurried in search of Melmoth. What had become of his predecessor?

The Englishman was living in a mansion in the Rue Férou, near Saint-Sulpice—a gloomy, dark, damp, and cold abode. The Rue Férou itself is one of the most dismal streets in Paris; it has a north aspect like all the streets that lie at right angles to the left bank of the Seine, and the houses are in keeping with the site. As Castanier stood on the threshold he found that the door itself, like the vaulted roof, was hung with black; rows of lighted tapers shone brilliantly as though some king were lying in state; and a priest stood on either side of a catafalque that had been raised there.

"There is no need to ask why you have come, sir," the old hall porter said to Castanier; "you are so like our poor dear master that is gone. But if you are his brother, you have come too late to bid him good-by. The good gentleman died the night before last."

"How did he die?" Castanier asked of one of the priests.

"Set your mind at rest," said an old priest; he partly raised as he spoke the black pall that covered the catafalque.

Castanier, looking at him, saw one of those faces that faith has made sublime; the soul seemed to shine forth from every line of it, bringing light and warmth for other men, kindled by the unfailing charity within. This was Sir John Melmoth's confessor.

"Your brother made an end that men may envy, and that must rejoice the angels. Do you know what joy there is in heaven over a sinner that repents? His tears of penitence, excited by grace, flowed without ceasing; death alone checked them. The Holy Spirit dwelt in him. His burning words, full of lively faith, were worthy of the Prophet-King. If, in the course of my life, I have never heard a more dreadful confession than from the lips of this Irish gentleman, I have likewise never heard such fervent and passionate prayers. However great the measures of his sins may have been, his repentance has filled the abyss to overflowing. The hand of God was visibly stretched out above him, for he was completely changed, there was such heavenly beauty in his face. The hard eyes were softened by tears; the resonant voice that struck terror into those who heard it took the tender and compassionate tones of those who themselves have passed through deep humiliation. He so edified those who heard his words that some who had felt drawn to see the spectacle of a Christian's death fell on their knees as he spoke of heavenly things, and of the infinite glory of God, and gave thanks and praise to Him. If he is leaving no worldly wealth to his family, no family can possess a greater blessing than this that he surely gained for them, a soul among the blessed, who will watch over you all and direct you in the path to heaven."

These words made such a vivid impression upon Castanier that he instantly hurried from the house to the Church of Saint-Sulpice, obeying what might be called a decree of fate. Melmoth's repentance had stupefied him.

At that time, on certain mornings in the week, a preacher, famed for his eloquence, was wont to hold conferences, in the course of which he demonstrated the truths of the Catholic faith for the youth of a generation proclaimed to be indifferent in matters of belief by another voice no less eloquent than his own. The conference had been put off to a later hour on account of Melmoth's funeral, so Castanier arrived just as the great preacher was epitomizing the proofs of a future existence of happiness with all the charm of eloquence and force of expression which have made him famous. The seeds of divine doctrine fell into a soil prepared for them in the old dragoon, into whom the Devil had glided. Indeed, if there is a phenomenon well attested by experience, is it not the spiritual phenomenon commonly called "the faith of the peasant"? The strength of belief varies inversely with the amount of use that a man has made of his reasoning faculties. Simple people and soldiers belong to the unreasoning class. Those who have marched through life beneath the banner of instinct are far more ready to receive the light than minds and hearts overwearied with the world's sophistries.

Castanier had the southern temperament; he had joined the army as a lad of sixteen, and had followed the French flag till he was nearly forty years old. As a common trooper, he had fought day and night, and day after day, and, as in duty bound, had thought of his horse first, and of himself afterwards. While he served his military apprenticeship, therefore, he had but little leisure in which to reflect on the destiny of man, and when he became an officer he had his men to think of. He had been swept from battlefield to battlefield, but he had never thought of what comes after death. A soldier's life does not demand much thinking. Those who cannot understand the lofty political ends involved and the interests of nation and nation; who cannot grasp political schemes as well as plans of campaign and combine the science of the tactician with that of the administrator, are bound to live in a state of ignorance; the most boorish peasant in the most backward district in France is scarcely in a worse case. Such men as these bear the brunt of war, yield passive obedience to the brain that directs them, and strike down the men opposed to them as the woodcutter fells timber in the forest. Violent physical exertion is succeeded by times of inertia, when they repair the waste. They fight and drink, fight and eat, fight and sleep, that they may the better deal hard blows; the powers of the mind are not greatly exercised in this turbulent round of existence, and the character is as simple as heretofore.

When the men who have shown such energy on the battlefield return to ordinary civilization, most of those who have not risen to high rank seem to have acquired no ideas, and to have no aptitude, no capacity, for grasping new ideas. To the utter amazement of a younger generation, those who made our armies so glorious and so terrible are as simple as children, and as slow-witted as a clerk at his worst, and the captain of a thundering squadron is scarcely fit to keep a merchant's day-book. Old soldiers of this stamp, therefore, being innocent of any attempt to use their reasoning faculties, act upon their strongest impulses. Castanier's crime was one of those matters that raise so many questions, that, in order to debate about it, a moralist might call for its "discussion by clauses," to make use of a parliamentary expression.

Passion had counseled the crime; the cruelly irresistible power of feminine witchery had driven him to commit it; no man can say of himself, "I will never do that," when a siren joins in the combat and throws her spells over him.

So the word of life fell upon a conscience newly awakened to the truths of religion which the French Revolution and a soldier's career had forced Castanier to neglect. The solemn words, "You will be happy or miserable for all eternity!" made but the more terrible impression upon him, because he had exhausted earth and shaken it like a barren tree; because his desires could effect all things, so that it was enough that any spot in earth or heaven should be forbidden him, and he forthwith thought of nothing else. If it were allowable to compare such great things with social follies, Castanier's position was not unlike that of a banker who, finding that his all-powerful millions cannot obtain for him an entrance into the society of the noblesse, must set his heart upon entering that circle, and all the social privileges that he has already acquired are as nothing in his eyes from the moment when he discovers that a single one is lacking.

Here was a man more powerful than all the kings on earth put together; a man who, like Satan, could wrestle with God Himself; leaning against one of the pillars in the Church of Saint-Sulpice, weighed down by the feelings and thoughts that oppressed him, and absorbed in the thought of a Future, the same thought that had engulfed Melmoth.

"He was very happy, was Melmoth!" cried Castanier. "He died in the certain knowledge that he would go to heaven."

In a moment the greatest possible change had been wrought in the cashier's ideas. For several days he had been a devil, now he was nothing but a man; an image of the fallen Adam, of the sacred tradition embodied in all cosmogonies. But while he had thus shrunk to manhood, he retained a germ of greatness, he had been steeped in the Infinite. The power of hell had revealed the divine power. He thirsted for heaven as he had never thirsted after the pleasures of earth, that are so soon exhausted. The enjoyments which the fiend promises are but the enjoyments of earth on a larger scale, but to the joys of heaven there is no limit. He believed in God, and the spell that gave him the treasures of the world was as nothing to him now; the treasures themselves seemed to him as contemptible as pebbles to an admirer of diamonds; they were but gewgaws compared with the eternal glories of the other life. A curse lay, he thought, on all things that came to him from this source. He sounded dark depths of painful thought as he listened to the service performed for Melmoth. The *Dies iræ* filled him with awe; he felt all the grandeur of that cry of a repentant soul trembling before the Throne of God. The Holy Spirit, like a devouring flame, passed through him as fire consumes straw.

The tears were falling from his eyes when—"Are you a relation of the dead?" the beadle asked him.

"I am his heir," Castanier answered.

"Give something for the expenses of the services!" cried the man.

"No," said the cashier. (The Devil's money should not go to the Church.)

"For the poor!"

"No."

"For repairing the Church!"

"No."

"The Lady Chapel!"

"No."

"For the schools!"

"No."

Castanier went, not caring to expose himself to the sour looks that the irritated functionaries gave him.

Outside, in the street, he looked up at the Church of Saint-Sulpice. "What made people build the giant cathedrals I have seen in every country?" he asked himself. "The feeling shared so widely throughout all time must surely be based upon something."

"Something! Do you call God *something*?" cried his conscience. "God! God! God!…"

The word was echoed and reëchoed by an inner voice, till it overwhelmed him; but his feeling of terror subsided as he heard sweet distant sounds of music that he had caught faintly before. They were singing in the church, he thought, and his eyes scanned the great doorway. But as he listened more closely, the sounds poured upon him from all sides; he looked round the square, but there was no sign of any musicians. The melody brought visions of a distant heaven and far-off gleams of hope; but it also quickened the remorse that had set the lost soul in a ferment. He went on his way through Paris, walking as men walk who are crushed beneath the burden of their sorrow, seeing everything with unseeing eyes, loitering like an idler, stopping without cause, muttering to himself, careless of the traffic, making no effort to avoid a blow from a plank of timber.

Imperceptibly repentance brought him under the influence of the divine grace that soothes while it bruises the heart so terribly. His face came to wear a look of Melmoth, something great, with a trace of madness in the greatness. A look of dull and hopeless distress, mingled with the excited eagerness of hope, and, beneath it all, a gnawing sense of loathing for all that the world can give. The humblest of prayers lurked in the eyes that saw with such dreadful clearness. His power was the measure of his anguish. His body was bowed down by the fearful storm that shook his soul, as the tall pines bend before the blast. Like his predecessor, he could not refuse to bear the burden of life; he was afraid to die while he bore the yoke of hell. The torment grew intolerable.

At last, one morning, he bethought himself how that Melmoth (now among the blessed) had made the proposal of an exchange, and how that he had accepted it; others, doubtless, would follow his example; for in an age proclaimed, by the inheritors of the eloquence of the Fathers of the Church, to be fatally indifferent to religion, it should be easy to find a man who would accept the conditions of the contract in order to prove its advantages.

"There is one place where you can learn what kings will fetch in the market; where nations are weighed in the balance and systems appraised; where the value of a government is stated in terms of the five-franc piece; where ideas and beliefs have their price, and everything is discounted; where God Himself, in a manner, borrows on the security of His revenue of souls, for the Pope has a running account there. Is it not there that I should go to traffic in souls?"

Castanier went quite joyously on 'Change, thinking that it would be as easy to buy a soul as to invest money in the Funds. Any ordinary person would have feared ridicule, but Castanier knew by experience that a desperate man takes everything seriously. A prisoner lying under sentence of death would listen to the madman who should tell him that by pronouncing some gibberish he could escape through the keyhole; for suffering is credulous, and clings to an idea until it fails, as the swimmer borne along by the current clings to the branch that snaps in his hand.

Toward four o'clock that afternoon Castanier appeared among the little knots of men who were transacting private business after 'Change. He was personally known to some of the brokers; and while affecting to be in search of an acquaintance, he managed to pick up the current gossip and rumors of failure.

"Catch me negotiating bills for Claparon & Co., my boy. The bank collector went round to return their acceptances to them this morning," said a fat banker in his outspoken way. "If you have any of their paper, look out."

Claparon was in the building, in deep consultation with a man well known for the ruinous rate at which he lent money. Castanier went forthwith in search of the said Claparon, a merchant who had a reputation for taking heavy risks that meant wealth or utter ruin. The money lender walked away as Castanier came up. A gesture betrayed the speculator's despair.

"Well, Claparon, the bank wants a hundred thousand francs of you, and it is four o'clock; the thing is known, and it is too late to arrange your little failure comfortably," said Castanier.

"Sir!"

"Speak lower," the cashier went on. "How if I were to propose a piece of business that would bring you in as much money as you require?"

"It would not discharge my liabilities; every business that I ever heard of wants a little time to simmer in."

"I know of something that will set you straight in a moment," answered Castanier; "but first you would have to—"

"Do what?"

"Sell your share of Paradise. It is a matter of business like anything else, isn't it? We all hold shares in the great Speculation of Eternity."

"I tell you this," said Claparon angrily, "that I am just the man to lend you a slap in the face. When a man is in trouble, it is no time to play silly jokes on him."

"I am talking seriously," said Castanier, and he drew a bundle of notes from his pocket.

"In the first place," said Claparon, "I am not going to sell my soul to the Devil for a trifle. I want five hundred thousand francs before I strike—"

"Who talks of stinting you?" asked Castanier, cutting him short. "You should have more gold than you could stow in the cellars of the Bank of France."

He held out a handful of notes. That decided Claparon.

"Done," he cried; "but how is the bargain to be made?"

"Let us go over yonder, no one is standing there," said Castanier, pointing to a corner of the court.

Claparon and his tempter exchanged a few words, with their faces turned to the wall. None of the onlookers guessed the nature of this by-play, though their curiosity was keenly excited by the strange gestures of the two contracting parties. When Castanier returned, there was a sudden outburst of amazed exclamation. As in the Assembly where the least event immediately attracts attention, all faces were turned to the two men who had caused the sensation, and a shiver passed through all beholders at the change that had taken place in them.

The men who form the moving crowd that fills the Stock Exchange are soon known to each other by sight. They watch each other like players round a card table. Some shrewd observers can tell how a man will play and the condition of his exchequer from a survey of his face; and the Stock Exchange is simply a vast card table. Everyone, therefore, had noticed Claparon and Castanier. The latter (like the Irishman before him) had been muscular and powerful, his eyes were full of light, his color high. The dignity and power in his face had struck awe into them all; they wondered how old Castanier had come by it; and now they beheld Castanier divested of his power, shrunken, wrinkled, aged, and feeble. He had drawn Claparon out of the crowd with the energy of a sick man in a fever fit; he had looked like an opium eater during the brief period of excitement that the drug can give; now, on his return, he seemed to be in the condition of utter exhaustion in which the patient dies after the fever departs, or to be suffering from the horrible prostration that follows on excessive indulgence in the delights of narcotics. The infernal power that had upheld him through his debauches had left him, and the body was left unaided and alone to endure the agony of remorse and the heavy burden of sincere repentance. Claparon's troubles everyone could guess; but Claparon reappeared, on the other hand, with sparkling eyes, holding his head high with the pride of Lucifer. The crisis had passed from the one man to the other.

"Now you can drop off with an easy mind, old man," said Claparon to Castanier.

"For pity's sake, send for a cab and for a priest; send for the curate of Saint-Sulpice!" answered the old dragoon, sinking down upon the curbstone.

The words "a priest" reached the ears of several people, and produced uproarious jeering among the stockbrokers, for faith with these gentlemen means a belief that a scrap of paper called a mortgage represents an estate, and the List of Fundholders is their Bible.

"Shall I have time to repent?" said Castanier to himself, in a piteous voice, that impressed Claparon.

A cab carried away the dying man; the speculator went to the bank at once to meet his bills; and the momentary sensation produced upon the throng of business men by the sudden change on the two faces, vanished like the furrow cut by a ship's keel in the sea. News of the greatest importance kept the attention of the world of commerce on the alert; and when commercial interests are at stake, Moses might appear with his two luminous horns, and his coming would scarcely receive the honors of a pun; the gentlemen whose business it is to write the Market Reports would ignore his existence.

When Claparon had made his payments, fear seized upon him. There was no mistake about his power. He went on 'Change again, and offered his bargain to other men in embarrassed circumstances. The Devil's bond, "together with the rights, easements, and privileges appertaining thereunto,"—to use the expression of the notary who succeeded Claparon, changed hands for the sum of seven hundred thousand francs. The notary in his turn parted with the agreement with the Devil for five hundred thousand francs to a building contractor in difficulties, who likewise was rid of it to an iron merchant in consideration of a hundred thousand crowns. In fact, by five o'clock people had ceased to believe in the strange contract, and purchasers were lacking for want of confidence.

At half-past five the holder of the bond was a house painter, who was lounging by the door of the building in the Rue Feydeau, where at that time stockbrokers temporarily congregated. The house painter, simple fellow, could not think what was the matter with him. He "felt all anyhow"; so he told his wife when he went home.

The Rue Feydeau, as idlers about town are aware, is a place of pilgrimage for youths who for lack of a mistress bestow their ardent affection upon the whole sex. On the first floor of the most rigidly respectable domicile therein dwelt one of those exquisite creatures whom it has pleased heaven to endow with the rarest and most surpassing beauty. As it is impossible that they should all be duchesses or queens (since there are many more pretty women in the world than titles and thrones for them to adorn), they are content to make a stockbroker or a banker happy at a fixed price. To this good-natured beauty, Euphrasia by name, an unbounded ambition had led a notary's clerk to aspire. In short, the second clerk in the office of Maître Crottat, notary, had fallen in love with her, as youth at two and twenty can fall in love. The scrivener would have murdered the Pope and run amuck through the whole sacred college to procure the miserable sum of a hundred louis to pay for a shawl which had turned Euphrasia's head, at which price her waiting woman had promised that Euphrasia should be his. The infatuated youth walked to and fro under Madame

Euphrasia's windows, like the polar bears in their cage at the Jardin des Plantes, with his right hand thrust beneath his waistcoat in the region of the heart, which he was fit to tear from his bosom, but as yet he had only wrenched at the elastic of his braces.

"What can one do to raise ten thousand francs?" he asked himself. "Shall I make off with the money that I must pay on the registration of that conveyance? Good heavens! my loan would not ruin the purchaser, a man with seven millions! And then next day I would fling myself at his feet and say, 'I have taken ten thousand francs belonging to you, sir; I am twenty-two years of age, and I am in love with Euphrasia—that is my story. My father is rich, he will pay you back; do not ruin me! Have not you yourself been twenty-two years old and madly in love?' But these beggarly landowners have no souls! He would be quite likely to give me up to the public prosecutor, instead of taking pity upon me. Good God! if it were only possible to sell your soul to the Devil! But there is neither a God nor a Devil; it is all nonsense out of nursery tales and old wives' talk. What shall I do?"

"If you have a mind to sell your soul to the Devil, sir," said the house painter, who had overheard something that the clerk let fall, "you can have the ten thousand francs."

"And Euphrasia!" cried the clerk, as he struck a bargain with the devil that inhabited the house painter.

The pact concluded, the frantic clerk went to find the shawl, and mounted Madame Euphrasia's staircase; and as (literally) the devil was in him, he did not come down for twelve days, drowning the thought of hell and of his privileges in twelve days of love and riot and forgetfulness, for which he had bartered away all his hopes of a paradise to come.

And in this way the secret of the vast power discovered and acquired by the Irishman, the offspring of Maturin's brain, was lost to mankind; and the various Orientalists, Mystics, and Archaeologists who take an interest in these matters were unable to hand down to posterity the proper method of invoking the Devil, for the following sufficient reasons:—

On the thirteenth day after these frenzied nuptials the wretched clerk lay on a pallet bed in a garret in his master's house in the Rue Saint-Honoré. Shame, the stupid goddess who dares not behold herself, had taken possession of the young man. He had fallen ill; he would nurse himself; misjudged the quantity of a remedy devised by the skill of a practitioner well known on the walls of Paris, and succumbed to the effects of an overdose of mercury. His corpse was as black as a mole's back. A devil had left unmistakable traces of its passage there; could it have been Ashtaroth?

* * * *

"The estimable youth to whom you refer has been carried away to the planet Mercury," said the head clerk to a German demonologist who came to investigate the matter at first hand.

"I am quite prepared to believe it," answered the Teuton.

"Oh!"

"Yes, sir," returned the other. "The opinion you advance coincides with the very words of Jacob Boehme. In the forty-eighth proposition of *The Threefold Life of Man* he says that 'if God hath brought all things to pass with a *let there be*, the *fiat* is the secret matrix which comprehends and apprehends the nature which is formed by the spirit born of Mercury and of God.'"

"What do you say, sir?"

The German delivered his quotation afresh.

"We do not know it," said the clerks.

"*Fiat?...*" said a clerk. "*Fiat lux!*"

"You can verify the citation for yourselves," said the German. "You will find the passage in the *Treatise of the Threefold Life of Man*, page 75; the edition was published by M. Migneret in 1809. It was translated into French by a philosopher who had a great admiration for the famous shoemaker."

"Oh! he was a shoemaker, was he?" said the head clerk.

"In Prussia," said the German.

"Did he work for the King of Prussia?" inquired a Boeotian of a second clerk.

"He must have vamped up his prose," said a third.

"That man is colossal!" cried the fourth, pointing to the Teuton.

That gentleman, though a demonologist of the first rank, did not know the amount of devilry to be found in a notary's clerk. He went away without the least idea that they were making game of him, and fully under the impression that the young fellows regarded Boehme as a colossal genius.

"Education is making strides in France," said he to himself.